DISTANT
DREAMS

ALICIA RADES

Published by Crystallite Publishing.

Produced in the United States of America.

Cover design by SelfPubBookCovers.com/Shardel

ISBN: 978-0-9974862-2-3

To my husband, Paul, who refuses to let me give up on my dreams.

1

I tell everyone my dream books are about the places I want to visit someday, but that's a lie. The books are filled with pictures of the places I've already been. Who would believe that, though? Kai Watson, a girl who has never physically left the Midwest, claims to have seen most of the world by age sixteen? It just doesn't make sense, and that's why I'll take the secret of my astral travels to the grave.

Each night is a new journey for me. Still, I never expected my travels to spark *this* kind of adventure. It started the night I chose to visit Yalong Bay in China. While everyone else was at the homecoming dance, I was preparing to travel the world. Savannah wanted me to go to the dance with her, but I couldn't bring myself to attend without a date. It's not like she had a date either, but I knew for a fact she'd find some guy to run off with and leave me sitting in a corner alone.

"You're missing out on the high school experience," she'd told me, but I didn't care. I was traveling the world.

The image of the blue ocean printed clearly. I pulled it from the printer's tray and placed it in the next slot of my photo album. *That's where I'm going tonight*, I thought proudly while admiring the gradient of the blue sea.

Braden burst into the room without warning. I quickly slammed the book shut as if I'd done something wrong. My eyes narrowed at my little brother in annoyance.

He stared me down. "Mom said you know where the TV remote is." Before I had a chance to answer, his gaze locked on my dream book. "Why are you still playing around with that stuff? How many do you have now, like ten?" His eyes drifted to the row of books on my shelf.

I nodded shyly.

My brother scoffed. "It would take you, like, thirty years to visit all those places, even if by some miracle you could afford the fastest jet in the world."

Braden would never know I didn't need a jet to get to those places. My means of travel were much quicker. But this was a prime example of why I couldn't tell anyone. No one would believe I could lucidly travel in my sleep.

"It's just for fun," I answered, hoping he couldn't

see the lie written all over my face. "It's not like it's ever going to happen."

Braden seemed to grow bored with this argument and simply stared at me blankly for several long seconds. "The remote?"

I rolled my eyes. "Aren't you supposed to be going to bed?"

"Mom says I can watch one episode," he told me before childishly sticking his tongue in my direction.

"It's on top of the TV." I paused briefly. Before he had a chance to turn to leave, I spoke again. "And seriously, knock next time. You never know when you might walk in on my naked butt."

A look of disgust crossed his face, but it was enough to make him flee at the thought.

I smiled triumphantly. *Now it's time for some peace and quiet*, I thought. I crawled into bed and pulled the covers over my body, settling in for another night of traveling the world. I twirled my dream catcher pendant around in my fingers before closing my eyes and drifting off.

I didn't truly fall asleep the way most people did — at least, my mind didn't. Once my body relaxed enough, I crawled out of it. In my spiritual state, I stood at my bedside and looked down at my sleeping body. My chest rose and fell slowly.

I closed my eyes — not my physical eyes since those were already closed, but my spiritual eyes that felt like they were there but really weren't. An image of Yalong

Bay came to mind. At first, the image was still, like the one I'd just printed out, but as I focused, it slowly became animated until waves were crashing against the shore and voices came into focus.

When I opened my eyes, I was standing at the edge of the ocean, and the sun shone bright above me. It was the sunlight that kept me mostly traveling to the Eastern Hemisphere, although I'd been known to nap during the day to explore attractions closer to home. It was frustrating at times that my travels were pretty much limited to those across the world. Actually, there were a lot of frustrating things about my travels. What I really wanted was to experience it first-hand, to physically visit each location.

My eyes journeyed downward to admire the sand at my feet. I dug my toes into it, except the sand didn't move around them. I sighed disappointedly. I closed my eyes again, conjuring up an image of a green bikini to replace my pajamas. I lay back in the sand to bask in the sun. My breathing slowed as I enjoyed the imaginary heat on my face. It almost felt real.

I must have lain there for hours. It's not like I had anything better to do. I let my mind wander to the point where it almost felt like I *was* dreaming, but I wasn't. I was in a real place, in real time, with real people, only none of them could see me.

When I finally decided to move, I looked around and took note of children playing in the sand, really touching it and interacting with it. I witnessed couples holding hands, experiencing the scene together. With how I traveled, I couldn't have any of that, and I desperately longed for it. The unexpected emotion that rippled through my body in that moment felt like a punch to the gut. Suddenly, this trip didn't seem worth it if I couldn't share it with someone else.

I decided I'd been lying in the sand long enough. I let my lids fall shut again. When I opened them, I was back in my bedroom, once again clothed in my pajamas. I glanced at the clock and noticed it was almost two a.m. My gaze shifted to my sleeping body on the bed. *If only I could bring my body with me on my travels*, I thought. Disappointment washed over me once again. *That's never going to happen.*

My family wasn't the most financially stable. I'd picked up a job at the grocery store as soon as I turned sixteen my sophomore year. I intended to save up money to travel after high school. It wasn't much money, though. I only worked two hours on weekdays and part-time on weekends. At the very least, my savings would give me a head start, and then I could make money as a travel blogger or something. At the rate things were going, though, I wasn't sure that would ever happen. Mom liked to "borrow" money from me every chance she got. Of course, she never paid it back. If my family actually had money like Darla Baxter's or Tiana King's, maybe I could bring my dreams of traveling *for real* to life.

Unfortunately, that's all my current travels were.

Dreams—of some sort, at least.

I didn't really want to be alone at the moment, but I didn't need the reminder from happy families and vacationing couples that I could never bring someone with me, not with the way I traveled.

Before I really knew what I was doing, I headed to the front door. I didn't *need* to leave through the front door. I could walk straight through my bedroom wall or even close my eyes and visualize my destination and be there in a snap, but I guess habit got the better of me. Besides, I didn't even know where I was headed. I stepped through the door as if I were a ghost. For several minutes, I didn't know where I was going until I realized I was walking my running route.

I didn't run tonight, though. I needed to kill time, and jogging wouldn't make it any easier. Nonetheless, that didn't stop my *mind* from running. On one level, I considered myself lucky to have this gift. On the other, its limitations only angered me.

When I reached the edge of the bluff, my frustration eased. This was always my favorite part of my jogging route. It was especially pretty this time of year when the leaves were beginning to change color and the trail up the slope was overtaken by mesmerizing fall colors. I couldn't see the colors now, not after I'd escaped the glow of the street lamps. Most of the time, that would bother me, but not on this path. I knew every rock and root well enough that the soft illumination from the moon was all I needed to guide my way.

I emerged from the woods when I reached the top of the bluff. There was a parking lot on the other side of a clump of trees to my left, but I had taken the road less traveled, up a trail that had been beaten down over the years by hikers and runners like me.

The empty clearing left me feeling lonely. In that moment, my thoughts flickered to Savannah. The dance would be over by now, but surely she'd still be having fun somewhere in a pretty dress. I nearly regretted not going with her. I closed my eyes and conjured up an image of a gorgeous purple full-length gown made of silk. I relaxed for a moment, feeling beautiful in my imaginary transformation. That, however, didn't make me feel any better about my gift.

Without visualizing a new outfit, I crossed the expansive clearing in the gown and stepped to the edge of the cliff. Water flowed in the river below me. Normally, I'd be freaked out being this close to the edge, but I knew no harm could come to me in this state. If I fell when I was in my body, there was a good chance I'd hurt myself in some way. If I fell like this, I'd simply be jolted awake. That's why I didn't mind hanging my feet off the edge. As soon as I took a seat and had a moment to think, annoyance returned and sizzled in my bones.

I fell onto my back, my toes still dangling off the edge of the cliff. *I just want to get out of this tiny town*, I thought. I wanted to truly touch the sand on the beach and let it fall through my fingers. I wanted to share that experience with someone. Unfortunately, I couldn't do that unless I traveled for real and took my body with me.

A shrill cry cut through my thoughts.

I jolted to my feet quickly, immediately alert. I couldn't tell where the sound had come from, so I didn't move right away. Then another scream resonated from somewhere near the parking lot.

"What the..." My words drifted off.

A third shriek sent me running toward the source. Someone was in trouble. It's not like I could do anything about it, but instinct overcame me. I pushed through the trees. When they began to thin, I slowed and crouched low. I don't know why I did. No one could see me, but I guess that didn't register in my mind at the moment.

My eyes locked on a bush where the sound of shuffling bodies and weak coughing was coming from. A thud came, throwing long brown hair into view. The girl's head smashed into the ground violently. She let out a grunt, but it was barely audible.

All I could do was stare in horror at the scene unfolding before my eyes. My heart slammed against my rib cage, and my lungs burned in protest to the breath I was holding.

Then, before I could manage to breathe, a rock came down on the girl's skull. Blood oozed from a fresh wound. One more time a concealed figure cracked the rock against the girl's forehead. It was only when she went limp and her head swiveled in my direction that I saw her eyes. They stared my way lifelessly while blood trickled down her familiar face.

A shriek of horror ripped out of my lungs. Before I could really process what I had just seen, the bluff washed away from my vision. I felt my spirit spring back to my body as if they were connected by elastic. I bolted upright in bed, my heart hammering. I didn't even realize I was truly screaming until my mother burst into my bedroom.

"What's going *on*?" she demanded.

I forced myself to swallow the bile rising in my throat without answering her. After a few moments, I finally realized what had just happened. I'd just witnessed Darla Baxter's murder, and I had no idea who killed her.

2

I hadn't slept the rest of the night, but that was no excuse to skip work. Sure, finding myself witness to a crime may have gotten me off the hook, but how could I possibly explain that to anyone? I couldn't exactly call up my boss and say, "Look, I can't make it in today because I was astral traveling last night and watched one of my classmates get murdered. I'm kind of traumatized by it."

Yeah, I don't think that would go over well. And how else could I possibly explain what I was doing up at the bluff so late when everyone knew I had been at home sleeping? It's not like I could say I changed my mind about the homecoming dance and snuck out of the house. My mom and my brother woke to my screams at the same time it happened.

I had convinced my family it was a bad dream— which I was still hoping it was—but I didn't think they'd be forgetting that my "nightmare" woke them at two a.m. anytime soon.

"Kai," my co-worker must have said for the third time.

I finally looked at her and stood up a little straighter behind my register. I didn't even know where I'd been staring.

"Are you okay?" she asked.

"Sorry, Meg. I didn't get enough sleep last night." At least that was the truth.

"Tell me about it." Megara—Meg for short—rolled her eyes in a gesture of agreement. She stood about five-foot-two and looked younger than me, even though she was a good eight years older. "My son was up all night puking. Anyway, would you mind...?"

She didn't have to finish her sentence. I'd heard the crash a minute ago.

Meg stared at me with a pleading expression. "I'm busy right now."

I sighed. "It's alright."

"Thank you!"

"What aisle was it?"

"Aisle six," she said, pointing. "It was a jar of salsa this time."

She rushed off in the opposite direction while I abandoned the register and headed to gather the cleaning supplies.

As I began picking up the broken glass and wiping up the salsa, I was once again alone with my thoughts. I couldn't prevent them from drifting back to Darla. Why was it that I hadn't heard anything about her yet? Even though work was slow since not many people in our town shopped on Sunday, you'd think *someone* would have heard *something*. In a town like Amberg—which everyone I knew called "Hamburger," probably fueled by our one and only fast food place in town, Amberg Hamburg—a murder would be the hottest news in the last decade. So what did that mean?

Oh. I noticed as soon as I asked the question. It meant no one had found her yet. *Oh, God. If no one knows she's dead, will they find her? No, that's silly. I know. But if I'm the only one who knows, that means I have to tell someone, right?*

No, I decided almost immediately as I thought it. *I can't explain what I was doing there. No one would believe me.*

Explanations ran through my head. Maybe I could say I went on a late night run or that I fell asleep on the bluff and woke to a scream. Except none of that made any sense because my family knew I was home at that exact time. If I somehow concocted an explanation, *I* might become a suspect because I was there.

But Darla's killer deserves justice!

As soon as the thought played through my mind, so did an image of Darla's lifeless stare. I paused from my clean-up duties and closed my eyes, as if that would make it all go away. It only brought the image behind my lids to life. Darla's killer smashed the rock against her head once, twice. Then her body went limp. Even as the scenario reran in my head, I couldn't remember a thing about the murderer. He'd been hidden behind the bush.

That settles it, I thought. *I won't tell anyone.* I didn't know enough to really tell anyone anything, and they'd find her once someone went up to the bluff, which shouldn't be long because plenty of people jogged up there. I only hoped I'd dreamt it all, that I hadn't heard anything about Darla because she was, in fact, still alive, but hoping was futile. I hadn't had a real dream my entire life. I was pretty sure I wasn't going to start now. What I'd seen had been real, and there was no denying it.

A cough pulled me from my thoughts. I immediately sprang to attention, and my gaze flew up to the man standing above me. Okay, perhaps "man" wasn't the right word. I recognized him immediately. Collin Baxter. He was in my grade, and we'd been on the cross country team together until I didn't sign up this year so I could take this job. He was also Darla's younger brother.

My eyes widened. *His sister is dead!* That's all I could think at that moment while I stared up at him stupidly. *He doesn't even know!*

"I'm sorry," I finally managed to croak out, though my apology was barely audible. I quickly finished wiping down the area and moved out of his way so he could reach the corn chips I was blocking. After returned my cleaning supplies to their storage area, I hurried back to the register just as Collin was approaching the checkout counter.

"Did you find everything alright?" I asked quieter than I intended to.

"Yeah," he replied, almost as softly as I did. He didn't sound like his normal self, which was usually upbeat and all smiles.

I scanned his bag of chips and jar of nacho cheese and rang up his total. I once knew Collin better than I did now, and I remembered a time in cross country when he'd told our team that nachos were his comfort food.

I couldn't look in his eyes for fear that he'd see what I was thinking. *Your sister is dead!*

I should tell him, I thought. *No, wait. How could I explain that? But maybe he knows something, like who might be a viable suspect.*

As much as I wanted to say something, I couldn't bring myself to do it. Besides, hadn't I said I would stay out of it? Instead, all I could say was, "Paper or plastic?" He rushed from the grocery store so quickly after I bagged his items that even if I wanted to ask him anything about Darla, I wouldn't have had the chance.

I stared after him. As he disappeared, the knot in my chest finally eased.

"You could cut the tension in the room with a

knife," Meg's voice sounded from behind me.

I whirled around to face her. "What?"

"That kid—Collin, right? Did you two date or something?" Meg leaned against the corner of the next register casually.

"What? No." I spoke almost too quickly as I brushed a strand of red hair out of my face. "Why would you say that?"

"Well, that whole thing was...awkward."

"Didn't you say you were busy with something?" I asked, hoping she'd drop the subject. It *was* awkward, probably because he reminded me so much of what I'd witnessed last night.

"Did I?" Meg asked innocently, straightening up. "Oh, right. No, I just didn't want to clean up the salsa." An amused smile twitched at the corner of her lips.

I threw a pen near my register at her in jest.

The rest of the day passed by slowly. When I caught a glimpse out the window, I noticed it was raining. It was the perfect weather to reflect my mood. I kept expecting to receive a text from Savannah about Darla— if there was news about her, Savannah would know— but when her text finally came, she didn't mention Darla.

You totally missed out last night! Savannah's text said.

God, she was right. I probably wouldn't have had any fun, but at least the horrible images in my mind wouldn't be there.

Go on… I texted back.

I didn't have to worry about pulling my phone out during work because there was only one customer who was still browsing the aisles and my boss wasn't in today.

The dance was fun, and then I went to the after party.

Worry knotted in my stomach. Knowing Savannah, she got wasted last night. I only hoped nothing bad happened to her because of it. Why did I have to be so selfish? If I had been there, I could have kept an eye on her.

You're okay, right?

Of course I am! It was loads of fun.

Please don't tell me you got drunk.

Maybe a little, but don't worry. Nothing bad happened. I'll tell you more at school.

At least that eased my nerves a bit, but it did nothing to relieve my guilt. *Then again,* I thought, *if I had gone to the dance and party with her, I wouldn't have seen what I'd seen, and what if I'm the only one who can do something about it?*

I quickly pushed the thought from my mind. *I will not get involved with this!* I told myself. Yet that didn't keep me from thinking about it and scolding myself for my ever-changing mind.

I'd seen some horrible things while astral traveling, but never something like this. It was actually a somewhat traumatic experience that gave birth to my distance travels. When I was younger, my spirit always came out of my body at night. I can't explain why. I'd heard some people call it astral projection—which was the best word I had for it—but I'd never met anyone else on the astral plane or saw the future or anything. All I knew was that I could do it.

Anyway, I used to make my parents keep the TV on. They thought I couldn't sleep without the noise. I just wanted it to keep myself occupied. One night when I was twelve, I was watching cartoons late, and I heard my parents talking about their divorce. They either thought I was asleep or figured the TV would drown out their conversation, but it couldn't, not when my spirit was in the same room as them.

I couldn't believe it. I didn't want to accept that my parents were separating. I still remember the pain that shuttered through my body. I couldn't be around my parents, not when they were fighting. All I wanted to do was run away. I wished I could go to my grandma's house and seek comfort in her. I closed my eyes and pictured her living room, and when I opened them, I was there. That's when I realized I could control where I went.

A month later, my grandma died. Needless to say, the next few months weren't the happiest of my life, and that only drove me to travel more. I eventually fell in love with it, and that's when I started the dream books.

Even when I was little, it didn't take me long to realize that I was the only one who could astral travel. My family would sometimes talk about their dreams—

how strange and weird they were—and I knew my dreams were different. I'd never told a soul about it.

None of that mattered anymore, though. By the time I headed home from work, I still hadn't heard a word about Darla, and I was starting to seriously wonder if I had imagined it.

* * *

When I arrived home, I slammed the front door a bit too forcefully. "Woops," I muttered.

"*Somebody's* angry," Braden accused from the living room couch. He was sprawled across the whole thing and munching on...

"You snot!" I quickly lunged for the container of dip he was plunging his pretzels into.

"What are you doing?" he yelled back.

"This is for Mom's mashed potatoes!" I pulled the container protectively away from him. It was only French onion dip with bacon, but Mom and I had specifically bought it for her custom recipe.

"I was eating that," Braden cried.

"Kai," my mother scolded as she entered the room. "What's going on in here?"

"I—he." My gaze shifted between my mother and my brother. "Braden's eating the dip we bought for your mashed potatoes. You know, my favorite."

"That's not even how you make mashed potatoes," Braden sneered.

I had the sudden urge to stick my tongue out at him

the way he liked to do to me, but I didn't. "It's how *Mom* makes mashed potatoes."

"Well, it's not how *normal* people make them," Braden spat before diving for the dip again.

"Stop it!" My mom pushed between us before turning to me. "Kai, I told him he could eat it. It's about to expire, and I just don't have the time to make the mashed potatoes."

"What? I—" I quickly checked the expiration date. Sure enough, the package would expire tomorrow. Had it really been that long since we bought it? I'd make the potatoes myself, but I could never quite get them as good as Mom's. Had it really been that long since she cooked us a decent dinner that wasn't frozen pizza or a meal-in-a-box?

My mother placed her hands on her hips. "Hand it back to your brother, and you can both share."

I did as I was told but suddenly lost my appetite. I shrugged like it didn't matter, but it definitely did. It wasn't the mashed potatoes that was a big deal. It was the empty feeling in the pit of my stomach that made it feel like my mother didn't care about me and my feelings anymore, like she had forgotten. I rushed to my room so neither of them would notice the tears welling up in my eyes.

At least when I reached my bedroom, I could find solace in researching new places to visit tonight. I sat at my second-hand computer. It was an ancient laptop Mom had given me when she finally upgraded hers. It was slower than molasses, but at least it was compatible with the ten dollar printer I'd found at a garage sale a few summers ago.

I settled on visiting the Tarlo River National Park in Australia just because I'd never been there and thought it might be interesting to break away from some of the bigger crowds and explore the terrain.

I'd managed to push thoughts of Darla far from my mind as I crawled into bed that night. I hadn't thought about her since I got home, but as soon as I fell asleep, that all changed.

Something I couldn't quite pinpoint felt off. Maybe it was my sense of balance. Maybe it was my vision. I didn't know. I didn't have a moment to really think about it when I witnessed the scene before me. Darla Baxter's face came into view from behind a bush. A hand clutching a rock rose up before accelerating toward her hairline. One crack. Two cracks. Darla's head went limp, and her motionless eyes pointed in my direction.

The yelp that escaped my lips this time only lasted a split second, so no one rushed in to check on me. I sprang straight up in bed, and my hands quivered. I couldn't place what had just occurred. How could something like that happen two nights in a row? Did Darla make it out alive Saturday night only for the killer to come after her to finish the job tonight? How did I get up on the bluff anyway without controlling it?

Oh, God. That's when I realized my logic didn't

make any sense. I quickly put the pieces together and understood what the strange sensation I'd felt through it all was.

For the first time in my life, I'd had a real dream.

3

For the second night in a row, I couldn't sleep. That made it easier to accept Savannah's invitation for coffee in the morning. I didn't usually go with her because I didn't want to spend the money, but this morning, it didn't seem to matter. I had dreamt for real, and it was the strangest thing that had ever happened to me. It wasn't exactly a dream, though. It was more like a memory.

"Earth to Kai." Savannah snapped her fingers in front of my face. We were sitting across from each other in Amberg Hamburg, sipping on our coffee. Savannah ran her fingers through her hair. This week, it was black with blue tips. Like my mom, Savannah's mother was a cosmetologist. They even worked together at the only hair salon in town. Unlike my family, Savannah's actually had some money to spare since her dad was an accountant, and, well, I didn't have a dad to help out. Savannah took advantage of her mom's job and dyed her hair a new color practically every week.

"I'm sorry," I told her. "I just didn't sleep well last night. I like your hair, by the way."

"Thank you," she said, bouncing her hair in her hand before reaching over to play with mine. "You know, your red hair would look killer with some black stripes."

I swatted her hand away. "No, thanks."

She pouted for a second before composing herself.

"You know, Mr. Spears is going to have a fit if you keep your hair that color until the play," I pointed out.

Savannah was in the school play, *Enchanting*, which was a spoof of common fairy tales. Our school did two plays a year, and Savannah had made it her life goal to play a part in each one. She never stopped telling me that she hoped she'd take the lead our senior year, but for now, she was only playing a woodland creature. At least she looked cute in her deer costume.

I was pretty sure she'd rock any lead role she got. When she first met our director, Mr. Spears, she put on a British accent for a whole week and convinced him she was a foreign exchange student. Even so, Mr. Spears had this "seniority" thing going, so our fingers were crossed that Savannah would make the lead in one of the plays next year. Unfortunately, I couldn't join the cast because play practice ran through my work schedule. Still, I helped on the sets and costumes during the short break I had between school and work.

"Relax," Savannah insisted, rolling her eyes at me. "I'll dye it brown to match my costume next week."

After a second, her demeanor changed. She rested her face on her hands and batted her eyes at me. If I wasn't straight, that look might have worked on me. I knew for sure it worked on enough guys, though that attraction could be thanks in part to her ample cleavage she didn't mind showing off.

"So." Savannah stretched the word out as if it were spelled with twenty O's. "Are you ready to hear everything you missed at the homecoming happenings?"

On a typically day, I wouldn't care that much, but at least when I was listening to Savannah talk, I didn't have to worry about what I'd witnessed on the bluff.

"I do. I really do, but unfortunately, we're already running late. If we don't chug our coffees and get going, we're going to be late for first period."

Savannah's face fell into a fake pout. "Okay, I'll tell you some of it on the way, and then you'll have to listen to the rest at lunch, okay?"

"Agreed."

Amberg Hamburg was only two short blocks from the school, so Savannah didn't get a chance to tell me much before we went our separate ways. She detailed the list of guys who asked her to dance, along with the number of girls who complimented her dress. None of it surprised me. Savannah was one of the school's biggest flirts, so guys paid attention to her a lot. Ironically, girls got along with her, too, probably because she wasn't a total slut. I had to admit, she was easy to get along with.

But that wasn't the only reason I was friends with her. She was super fun to be around. I loved her like a sister, but I also knew that if I had any chance of getting out of this town, it was with someone as confident and determined as Savannah. The only thing that bothered me was that I couldn't quite figure out why she was friends with *me*. I mean, everyone liked her, and I basically tried to make myself as invisible as possible as I planned my escape from Amberg. I guess we grew close because our moms were friends. Savannah and I had been friends as long as I could remember.

Once Savannah and I headed to our own classes—we sadly only had seventh period math together this semester—there was nothing to distract me. I continued to wonder why there was no talk of Darla spreading around school. I could feel it in the atmosphere that *some* gossip was buzzing, but each time I rudely listened in, I never heard mention of Darla's name. I could only catch that something had happened with the homecoming king and queen.

At lunch, I finally got a chance to engage in the gossip.

"What's everyone so chatty about today?" I asked Savannah as soon as I took my seat.

"I told you I had a ton to tell you."

"About Anna and Hunter?" I asked. They were the homecoming king and queen, something I'd quickly picked up on throughout the day. From what I'd heard, it sounded like something went down between the two of them.

Savannah's eyes widened. "You haven't heard yet?"

I shook my head.

Savannah sat up straighter. No doubt she was happy to have me so interested in the gossip, which wasn't typical of me. "Okay, so you know I went to this after party. It was supposed to be super secret and everything, but tons of people were there." She drew in a deep breath. "Anyway, it's this sort of tradition at the party that someone blindfolds the king and queen at some point during the night and then puts them in a closet together. It's like Seven Minutes in Heaven or something."

She paused so I could absorb this. I'd heard of the tradition before and nodded for her to continue.

"As you may know, Anna has a boyfriend from out of town."

I didn't know that, but she continued without waiting for confirmation.

"Anna told her friends she didn't want to do it—to go in the closet with Hunter—and so when they blindfolded her and took her to the closet, she freaked out. She started hitting her friends and screaming. I was there. I saw the whole thing."

Something about this story sounded strangely familiar.

"Didn't something like that happen last year?" I asked.

Savannah shrugged. "There always seems to be some sort of drama at the after party, which is why I couldn't resist going."

"I'm surprised the police haven't noticed it happens every year and didn't go bust it up."

Savannah only shrugged again, but she overdid the motion like she was practicing for her future acting career. "I'm glad they didn't, because there's more! I've been dying to tell you this all day. Okay. Are you ready?" She paused for suspense.

I played along. "What is it?"

She lowered her voice and glanced around before leaning in closer to me to whisper. "Shawn Cameron kissed me."

I drew in a sharp breath before realizing she must be joking. I burst out laughing.

Savannah's brows came together, and her jaw dropped to exaggerate her offense. Every expression with her was an exaggeration. "What's so funny about that?"

I stopped laughing to assess her face. She was dead serious. "Oh. I'm sorry. I guess I just didn't believe it. You did say 'Shawn Cameron,' right?"

"Yeah."

"The most popular guy in school?" I clarified.

"He's not *the* most popular. Remember that Hunter won homecoming king."

"But *Shawn Cameron*? Was he drunk?"

Savannah's voice came out a few notes higher than normal. "Why is that so hard to believe?"

I shook my head with a laugh. "I guess I just never expected it." That was only half true. I totally expected her to hook up with someone, but I didn't think it'd be Shawn Cameron of all guys.

"Oh, you better believe it! With the way I looked last Saturday, the guys couldn't keep their eyes off me." Savannah tossed her hair over her shoulder dramatically.

"You mean they couldn't stop staring at your boobs," I corrected her.

A blush rose to Savannah's cheeks, a rarity for her. "Maybe."

"So, what was it like?" I teased.

"It was…" She stared off into the distance as if dreaming. "Magical," she finished. "He'd asked me to dance earlier in the night. Can you believe he didn't have a date? And neither did I—I like to keep my options open, you know?—so we sort of hung out. At the after party, we were hanging out near the music, and he just kind of did it and told me he liked me, that he's liked me for a long time." Savannah's face fell. "Sadly, nothing else happened. He got this phone call and had to leave."

"Are you sure he didn't just ditch you?"

"No way! I could tell someone was on the other end of the line. Besides, he couldn't take his eyes off me." Savannah flashed her award-winning smile. "You should have been there."

I bit the inside of my lip to silence my complaints, but Savannah must have caught onto my expression.

"I'm sorry," she said. "I know you don't really have the money for a dress."

I shrugged like it didn't matter. "I have *some* money. It's just that I'm trying to save it for when I get to go on my big adventure. I maybe would have bought a dress if my mom wasn't constantly 'borrowing' money from me." I gritted my teeth in annoyance.

"Come on, Kai. You have to let that go at some point. When is the last time she did that?"

Now that I thought about it, I couldn't really remember. "That doesn't mean she's paid me back."

"I offered for you to wear one of my dresses," Savannah said like my family issues weren't a big deal.

I nearly burst out laughing. "Can you imagine me trying to fit into one of your dresses designed to fit your double D's? Besides, I'm way taller than you, so any of them would have been too short."

"Oh, please. They're not that short. You could use showing off your legs. They're your best feature. You see, I have my chest. Shawn has his biceps. You're supposed to embrace the good things about yourself. Like how Shawn is *so* good at kissing." She smiled like it was a triumph to find a way to remind me of her hot kiss with Shawn.

When she turned back to her tray and began eating, I had a moment to let what she'd said settle in my mind. That's when I realized I had an opportunity to learn more about what happened to Darla.

"Didn't Shawn used to date Darla Baxter?" I asked casually.

"Yeah, for like, a year. Why?"

"She wasn't jealous when she saw you two kissing?" I applauded myself for my subtlety.

"Um...I don't remember her being in the general vicinity."

I bit my lip in thought. "She didn't go to the dance? That's weird."

"No, she did. She was on homecoming court. She must have just been in another room at the party when Shawn kissed me. I don't want to know what would have happened if she saw us kissing. I've heard she never really got over him."

"There's no other gossip on her?" I asked. Maybe she had a fight with someone at the dance. Maybe...Okay, I had no idea where I was going with this.

"Not that I heard. Wait, did you hear something?" Her face suddenly lit up.

"No. What time did the dance end again?"

Savannah eyed me. Dang it. I was losing my subtle touch.

"It went until midnight," she informed me.

Okay. That left two hours until I saw her murder. I wondered what she'd been doing during that time and who had been with her. Something else bothered me, too: the fact that no one was talking about it. Did that mean that I imagined it? Did that mean Darla was still alive? Or maybe it simply meant they hadn't found her yet. I mulled these thoughts over the following period, but the more I thought about it, the more I realized there was absolutely nothing I could do about it.

Forget it, I told myself. Sadly, I was selfish and heartless enough that I didn't worry about Darla the rest of the school day.

I couldn't say the same thing when I stepped into the auditorium to help with the set for the play. I had a half hour until I had to head to work, and at least painting made me feel useful. I quietly chatted with a few people I knew well: Tyler, who was one of the tech crew guys working with mics and lighting, and Lindsay, a student helping with costume design. As soon as Mr. Spears called the practice to order, I headed over to gather my painting supplies to help two other girls paint the castle backdrop. We had less than two weeks to finish up the set — the play opened next Friday — but I wasn't too worried.

What really bothered me was when I heard Tiana King begin to recite her lines. She was the epitome of beauty — big blue eyes, long blonde hair, and a smile that would win a beauty pageant. She was playing the lead role of Cinderella. I'd already heard her lines a million times because Savannah insisted on memorizing the lead role even though she was just an extra, but I knew she loved the practice.

When Tiana's voice filled the stage, a nervous twisting in my gut sprang to life. She wasn't just the lead in the play. She was also Darla Baxter's best friend, and that connection put Darla at the forefront of my mind for the next half hour.

As I listened to Tiana perform her lines, I couldn't help but think about how terrible it was that even Darla's best friend didn't know she was gone. For a second, it made me want to tell someone about Darla's death so she could rest in peace and her killer could be brought to justice. Then I had to remind myself that one, I didn't *really* know anything, and two, I couldn't do anything to change it.

4

After work, I suited up for my evening run the way I did almost every night. I pulled on my running pants, my favorite t-shirt, and my ratty old tennis shoes and took off. With the chilly wind rushing through my red ponytail, I was surprised at how good it felt to push forward on the pavement. I'd be on the cross country team if it wasn't for my job and the sliver of hope that I might still be able to save up *just* enough money to truly travel.

Although I was alone with my thoughts, it was easy to take my mind off everything when I was running. A sense of happiness filled my soul—the kind of happiness I felt when I thought about traveling. I ran partially because I loved it, but I also knew I had to stay in shape for when I finally hopped on a plane and found myself at the beginning of my epic adventure. I figured I'd start with a sport like skydiving or backpacking. Those were things I couldn't do in my dreams. They were true experiences, much in contrast to my normal passive observations.

My feet slapped against the deserted road, a sound that left me filled with a sense of accomplishment. I zigzagged through the streets of Amberg without really paying attention to my surroundings. My route took me mostly through residential areas and then out past the town cemetery. Although the bright fall leaves gave character to the rest of the town, the trees behind the gates of the cemetery appeared dull, like they knew death lay beneath them. The air grew chillier as I raced along the road, which sent an eerie sensation down my spine. I quickened my pace as I passed the grave markers. I knew I was being silly, but with Halloween approaching, I figured one could never be too careful around a graveyard. Who knew what lay out of sight?

Before I realized how far I'd come, I found myself at the base of the bluff. I slowed as I approached it and took a deep breath. I was partially terrified to go back there, but it's not like someone was *stalking* the bluff waiting for his next victim. At least, I prayed that wasn't the case.

I paced near the entrance to the trail and contemplated where I should go next. The truth was, curiosity won out. I had to take a look at the crime scene, to see if I had imagined it, to see if it happened for real.

I took off up the trail.

Although the sun was already low in the sky, I could make out the glorious array of colors in the trees. Yellow, orange, and red leaves swirled around me as I pushed up the path. My legs burned slightly, thanks to the steep incline, but I soon found myself breaking free of the trees and emerging into the clearing that stretched out to the edge of the cliff. For a moment, I stood there motionless. Now was the perfect time to marvel at the beauty of the changing fall leaves. If I had a camera, I'd come up here and photograph some of it as practice for my travel blog I was going to start in a couple of years, but all I had was the crappy camera on my second-hand prepaid phone.

I inched my way across the clearing but stopped at the wooden fence about five feet short of the edge. It wasn't really a fence or a guardrail but rather just a deterrent to keep people from getting too close to the edge. It didn't do much considering I'd seen plenty of people bravely cross it. I couldn't bring myself to get any closer, not when my mind was attached to my body. One misstep and I'd be a goner. After cooling down and enjoying the scenery, I finally remembered why I'd decided to come up the path when fear had been toying with me at the base of the bluff.

I followed the path from the clearing to the parking lot through the clump of trees. As soon as I spotted the parking lot, I noticed the bushes planted neatly around it. The area was tidy and well landscaped, and even though the sun was setting, there were a couple of cars still up here. No doubt the owners were strolling along some of the walking paths or bravely dangling their feet off the edge of the cliff.

I found my way to the tree I had hidden behind when I was in my spirit form. I crouched down to confirm the angle of the bush that now reminded me of death. *The bush of death*, I thought to myself. It was there, the exact same bush with the exact same tangled branches I had seen that night. How could I have imagined that? Even with this confirmation, I stepped closer to the bush cautiously, as if I thought Darla's killer would jump out from behind it and crack my skull open the way he had Darla's. But when the opposite side of the bush came into view, I saw nothing. Absolutely nothing. I didn't know what I was expecting, maybe to find the rock, or at the very least a blood stain, but the area was completely clear.

I sank to the ground and brought my knees to my chest, wondering what it all could mean. I glanced toward my hiding tree and then back at the bush. There's no way I could have dreamt what happened. *Something* would have been out of place in my imagination, yet something seemed to be missing here, too. No rock. No body. Not even a drop of blood.

Though I knew it was silly, I began picking up stray leaves that had blown across the manicured grass. I guess I expected to find some upturned dirt or something, but there was nothing. Then again, I wasn't an expert, so I didn't really know what to look for. My hands quivered as I combed the area, though I didn't have a clear explanation for why. Perhaps it was because I felt queasy knowing what had happened there or because I suddenly realized I was disturbing a crime scene.

Just as I leaned closer to the spot I was sure Darla's head had fallen, I heard the crunch of leaves behind me. My heart immediately jumped in my chest, and without bothering to look back, I leapt to my feet and took off down the long road that led up to the parking lot. I couldn't say why I had the sudden urge to flee, but the desire to get as far away as I could overcame me. Maybe it was because I was already terrified of snooping around—of what I might find—or maybe I started to believe that the idea of a serial killer stalking the bluff wasn't so far-fetched. Nonetheless, I hightailed my way out of there without looking back for even a second, and I made it home in record time.

I huffed harder than usual when I reached my house. I quickly flung the door shut and locked it behind me before bracing myself against it and finally slowing my breathing.

"Running from something?" a male voice asked.

My pulse quickened. The first thought that crossed my mind was *He's found me*. But when my eyes sprang open a split second later, I relaxed. It was only my mom's friend, Jack, although his posture was strange. The kitchen chair he sat in was pulled out from the table and pointed at the front door.

I swallowed deeply. "No. Just my normal run."

A second later, my mother emerged from the hallway into the main living area and crossed over to the kitchen, which was open to the living room.

"You're home a little early," she pointed out.

I checked the clock on the wall. Dang, I really had made it home fast, although I had cut a few zig-zags off my jog to make it back.

"Yeah, well, it's starting to get dark outside sooner, and I didn't want to be out at night," I lied.

My mother continued what she was doing while I spoke. She reached for a piece of fabric on the table and shook it out in her hands before wrapping it around Jack. No, not a piece of fabric. A cape.

I inched my way farther into the house. "You're— you're cutting Jack's hair?" I asked, hoping the hurt wasn't too evident in my tone.

"It's Officer Delaney," Jack corrected me.

He insisted I call him that—something about respecting authority—but I didn't see how that was fair considering Mom called him Jack all the time. Besides, "Jack" *fit* him better when he wasn't in uniform. He probably let my mom get away with it because he liked her. They'd been friends since high school but never dated. Now that they were both divorced, I couldn't see anything stopping them; although, I was glad he hadn't made a move because I did *not* want him as a step-father. I didn't need any more siblings in my life, either.

"Mm hmm," my mom nodded.

"But, Mom. I've been asking you to trim my hair for weeks," I complained. I tried not to sound too ungrateful in hopes that she'd offer to trim my hair after his. I pulled at my ponytail to inspect the fuzzy split ends and frowned at how damaged they looked.

"Your brother just heated up some fish sticks if you want some," my mom informed me. She gestured to the stove, leaving me with no such luck on the hair cutting offer.

I sulked over toward the cookie sheet of fish sticks. "Well, I hope Jack's paying you," I muttered, but neither of them heard me. It sickened me to see my mother giving Jack a free haircut when we were already tight on money and it was what my mom did for a living.

I reluctantly managed to eat the fish sticks, thanks greatly in part to Mount Ketchup, and then hurried off to my room. I couldn't stand watching Mom and Jack laugh together. Mom never laughed like that with me or Braden.

Braden stopped me in the hall, spreading his arms from one wall to the other.

"Get out of my way," I demanded through gritted teeth.

An evil grin spread across my brother's face. "What's the magic word?"

I let out a puff of air and rolled my eyes. "Please?"

"Nope," he said proudly.

I pursed my lips. "Just let me through!" I pushed at

his arms, but the darn kid was nearly as big as I was.

"What's the magic word?"

Normally we'd bicker longer, but I was already agitated. Without really thinking about doing it, I stomped on his bare foot and pushed past him when his guard was down.

"Ow!" he cried out. "Mom! Kai stomped on my foot."

"Kai," my mother and Jack both scolded in unison.

"Be nice to your brother," my mother's voice sounded through the hallway just before I swung my bedroom door shut.

Maybe my mom should just run off with Jack. I could go live with Savannah, and Braden could go live at his friend Zach's house.

I knew how childish my thoughts sounded at the moment, but I couldn't control my spite. It was silly to be mad over a stupid *haircut*, yet I felt completely justified in it. How could Mom never have time for her own kids yet she could spare plenty of time for Jack? It just wasn't fair. Nothing had been fair since my dad left us.

My dad. That thought was even worse. He only ever called on birthdays and Christmas. Braden still had this idea that Dad was going to show up one day, get down on one knee, and ask Mom to remarry him. Even if I could dream, I wouldn't have let *that* thought enter my wildest ones. Dad was never coming back, and sometimes it felt like Mom wished she could leave us, too.

I shook off thoughts of my parents and sat down at my computer. It's not like being mad at them on a constant basis would help anything. After tending to my social media accounts, Jack finally left, and I managed to venture my way back into the kitchen and load the dishwasher like a good little girl. I showered and then returned to my room and cozied in under my blankets.

Australia, here I come.

I closed my eyes and let my body relax. With no transition, I found myself at the top of the bluff, crouched down behind my hiding tree. Worry for how I'd gotten there without controlling it didn't even occur to me. Familiarity of the scene didn't register in my mind. It was like I was watching it for the first time.

I stared across the space toward the bush. Horror overcame me when Darla's skull knocked against the ground, bringing her face into view. A rock smashed against her head twice before her body went limp in the grass.

I jolted awake and noticed immediately how quick and shallow my breaths were. Before I could stop myself, tears began sliding down my cheeks. The pounding of my heart was nearly audible. Slowly, I relaxed as I took in my surroundings and realized I was safe in my own bedroom. Still, I couldn't shake the terror rising within my body.

Darla's death had frightened me enough, and it appeared as if the horror from that night had left scars I didn't even realize I'd had. Two nights in a row now I'd had a dream. I'd dreamt like everyone else.

And that's when the true horror struck. What if this meant I would never astral travel again?

5

I felt ill the rest of the night, but I managed to rest my eyes enough that I could do without the coffee. It's not like I needed to be fully awake to understand what was going on in class anyway. Even though I woke with enough confidence to drag my butt to school, I couldn't let go of the worry that taunted me throughout the day.

"Are you okay, Kai?" Savannah asked when we met up at our lockers. If she hadn't mentioned my name, I may not have processed anything she'd said.

"What?" I jerked my gaze toward her. "Yeah, I'm fine."

"You don't look fine. You look tired as hell. Did you sleep at *all* last night?"

I don't know. Did I? "I tried to," I managed to say.

"And the problem is…?" she prompted.

I sighed. "I've been having this nightmare." I could hardly believe the truth was coming out of my mouth. I hadn't intended to tell her, but it was a relief to have one less thing weighing on my shoulders.

"Oh? Care to enlighten me?" Savannah pulled her textbook across her chest as we headed to class.

"It's nothing really," I said with a shrug.

"You're such a liar," she accused.

I couldn't argue with that one. "I—" I paused for a second and glanced around. Then I grabbed Savannah's wrist and pulled her into the closest restroom. I quickly checked the stalls. We were alone.

I couldn't tell her what I saw. I knew that much. I would never breathe a detail of my gift, either. Even though she was my best friend, I had no idea how she'd take it. Would she think I was pranking her? Would she call me a freak? Would she hate me for waiting so long to tell her? I didn't want to find out, but I figured a slight hint at the truth wouldn't hurt.

"I've just been having really bad dreams and can't sleep, okay?" I knew that wouldn't convince her.

"What kind of dreams? Sexy vampire dreams?"

God, I wished. "No, Savannah. I'm serious. I can't sleep. I just keep dreaming of…death." I pressed my lips together. That's all I could say. I wasn't sure how Savannah would take any more honest details.

She blinked a few times. "Well, that's creepy. What do you think it means?"

I dropped my book onto the restroom counter and

turned toward the mirror. "What do I think it means? I don't know. That I'm afraid of something?" Well, that was the truth, but suddenly, I was regretting saying anything to Savannah.

"Oh, I know!" Her eyes lit up. "Maybe it means you need closure. You know, death is a sort of 'end,' so you need to end something."

I eyed her skeptically. Why did I have to be honest? "And what do you suggest that's about?"

She raised her eyebrows and twisted her lips to the side as if to say, *Like you don't know.*

I shot her a look back that said, *How should I?*

"Your dad," Savannah stated like it was obvious. "I know it sucks, but maybe you need closure from him leaving you guys."

I was about to protest and tell her I'd already found closure with my father and that I couldn't care less about him than he did of me. Instead, I readily agreed with her to prevent her from finding another imaginary scenario I needed closure from.

I quickly realized that mentioning my nightmares was a mistake, yet as I pushed through the halls to my first period class, I recognized there was some merit to Savannah's suggestion. Closure. Maybe if I found closure to Darla's death, the nightmares would end and I'd have my gift back.

Yes, that's it! A sense of pride overcame me before my following thoughts immediately shot that theory down. How was I going to find closure? To do that,

Darla's killer would have to be brought to justice, and how could *I* help with that? I couldn't go running to the cops and say I witnessed the murder, not when I didn't *really* see anything anyway. Maybe if I stumbled upon some evidence, they'd start investigating it. *Great idea, Kai, considering you don't know where to find the evidence.* Maybe if I'd just give it time, someone would realize she was gone.

Worry once again knotted in my gut. How had it been almost three days and no one noticed she was missing? And who could I ask about that? I was just Kai Watson. I wasn't friends with Darla. Would it look suspicious if I asked about her?

It turns out that I didn't have to. As soon as I took my seat in first period, I heard someone speak her name. Without turning my head, I focused my attention across the room and on the voice.

"She ran away," the girl said.

"Darla Baxter?" a guy asked. "I don't believe it. I thought she was just out sick. What does a girl like that have to run away from? She's popular and basically has everything anyone could ever dream of."

"I heard it was a secret boyfriend," another girl interjected. "She ran away with him."

"It's not the first time she's done this, either," the first girl said. "My cousin lives next door to the Baxters, and he told me that last summer she ran away and was gone for, like, a week. Her dad was apparently really pissed and made this huge scene on the front lawn when he found out."

My heart rate quickened. What if I was wrong about this whole thing? If what they were saying was true—that Darla ran away—then maybe I *did* just dream about the murder. Perhaps it's nothing more than what Savannah suggested, that I needed closure in my life. Except, why would I dream of Darla if I needed closure?

I pressed my face into my hands, not bothering if any of my classmates noticed my distress. Suddenly, I put the pieces together, and I dropped my hands. What if Darla had intended to run away but she never made it that far? What if the boyfriend they were talking about convinced her to run away with him but he killed her on the bluff before they ever left town? By the next day, he could have been long gone, and no one would know because he was a "secret" boyfriend.

But if he was secret, how did anyone know about him at all? Maybe he wasn't so secret after all. Maybe Darla's best friend knew about him. If Tiana King knew something, I could talk to her…

No. I don't need to do anything. They know she's gone now. Someone will find her.

Still, I couldn't help but wonder. I wasn't just desperate for closure for the sake of my gift anymore. The mystery of what all went down pulled me in like I was watching a horror movie that was sure to have some amazing plot twist at the end, the kind of movie you couldn't tear your eyes away from even though the storyline made you want to hurl.

This was exactly like that, except the horror was real.

* * *

I didn't know what I could do about this whole mystery on my own — probably nothing but sit around. It wasn't until lunch when I spotted Collin Baxter headed out the doors for open campus lunch that I realized something. Tiana King may not have been the only one who knew something about Darla's disappearance. Collin had to know something about her running away, not only because he was her brother but because I remembered how he acted the day after it all happened. He wasn't himself. He was down, sad, like he knew something had happened to his sister.

I couldn't just flat out ask him about it, though. I hadn't really talked to him since I'd quit the cross country team. Would it look weird if I suddenly struck up a conversation?

By the end of the day, I was seriously convinced I would stay out of it all. I figured now that the rumors were flying, people would get worried, and someone would discover the truth. Still, I couldn't let go of this idea that I needed to take action if I was to find the closure Savannah had been talking about.

* * *

Tiana's whiny voice pierced into my ears like it was somehow filled with poison. Sure, she was popular and

Darla's best friend, and I felt deeply for her loss, but I couldn't argue with Savannah that Tiana was annoying as hell — and not just because she got the part in the play that Savannah so desperately wanted.

I had just reached the stage after class and was gathering my painting supplies when I locked onto her voice. I couldn't exactly ignore her when she was just a couple of feet behind me.

"I want to wear the ball gown for the receiving line," Tiana complained to Mr. Spears.

"But the play ends with you in Cinderella's peasant clothing," Mr. Spears explained.

"I get that, but I think the audience would like the ball gown better. It's just so *pretty*."

Mr. Spears sighed in defeat. "It really does say 'Cinderella,' doesn't it? The thing is, I don't want you wasting any time." He raised his voice. "Hey, Kai!"

I swiveled around to face him. *Uh oh*.

"You'll be here for the play, right?"

I nodded. "That's the plan. I took off work."

"Perfect. You'll help Ms. King into her dress after curtain call."

I went silent for a second and shifted my gaze between the two of them.

"Look," Mr. Spears said, "if she's going to do a costume change for the receiving line, it has to be *quick*. You can help her, right?"

I'd be moving sets during scene changes, but it's not like I was doing anything else after curtain call. "Yeah, I can help."

Tiana plastered a friendly smile on her face that I was pretty sure was completely fake. "Thank you so much! Do you mind if I show you something quick before practice starts?"

I followed after her.

Tiana stopped in front of her ball gown that was hanging on one of the racks backstage. "There's this piece of fabric here." She pointed while gathering the dress in her hands to show me. "It tends to get caught in the zipper, so you have to make sure to push it out of the way when you zip the dress up, okay?"

I nodded uncomfortably. I wasn't one for talking to popular girls like Tiana, who no doubt joined the play to satisfy her innate need to be the center of attention, although the truth was, she *was* talented. I mean, I'd talked with plenty of mildly popular people who Savannah knew, but even Savannah wasn't close to the crowd Tiana normally hung with—though I guess that was changing now that Shawn Cameron had shown interest in Savannah.

"Why aren't you in the play?" Tiana asked with a light tone like she cared. "You'd make a great Ariel with your red hair. I mean, Christa is a great Ariel, but she just doesn't have the look, even with the wig, you know?"

I reflexively ran my fingers through the ends of my hair. "I, uh, have work at four, so I can't stick around for the full rehearsal," I explained.

"Oh, that's a shame."

Her words came out sounding super friendly, but like most girls in the popular crowd at our school, I knew there was a class-A bitch behind that smile. At least, I'd always thought so. Maybe Tiana wasn't that bad. After all, I knew Darla hadn't been a bitch, so maybe her best friend was just as good of a person as she was.

Oh, God. Did I just think of Darla in the past tense? The thought made me sick, but a bit of hope toyed with me, evening out my emotions. If Tiana was being nice to me, maybe I could learn more about Darla.

"Tiana," I said quickly before she could turn away and head back toward the main stage. I quickly glanced around and noticed no one near us. I put on my most friendly expression.

"Yeah?"

"Can I ask you something?"

She nodded, the smile on her face never wavering.

"I'm sorry if this sounds…I just…I know it's not my place, but I know you were best friends with Darla Baxter, and I was wondering if you knew what happened to her."

Tiana's smile quickly faded. "What makes you think I know what happened to her?"

Suddenly, I couldn't meet her gaze. "You were her best friend, right?" I nearly flinched when I realized that again I'd thought of Darla in the past tense.

"Yeah, I *was*." Even with her acting skills, Tiana

couldn't mask the edge to her tone. "That was a long time ago."

"Oh, I'm sorry," I said, still unable to meet her gaze.

"She ran away with some guy. That's all I know. That's all anyone knows."

Tiana quickly pushed past me, and I immediately regretted bringing up the topic. Someone had to know something, right? If not Tiana, then who?

6

I didn't know what I would accomplish by heading back up to the bluff after work, but I did know I wanted my abilities back. I knew I wanted all of this to be over. If no one knew anything about Darla, I figured I was the only one who could do anything. The thing was, I still couldn't explain what I had seen or how I had seen it. I thought maybe I could "stumble" upon something and bring it to the cops. I didn't know what that might be, but I couldn't ignore the pull of the bluff and my own curiosity to this mystery.

I jogged up the path and wandered back to the bush of death. I knew it was silly because I hadn't found anything there before, but I needed a place to start. From there, I could scan the area for a bloody rock or something. Maybe I'd find drag marks.

But as I approached the bush again, I realized how useless snooping around would be. There wasn't anything here, just like there wasn't anything here yesterday. Still, I couldn't keep myself from crouching down and inspecting the area closer. Nothing.

"Kai?" a male voice cut through my concentration.

I sprang to my feet and whirled around to face him. Collin Baxter stood a few yards from me. He was dressed in running shorts, like me, with a gray t-shirt that was far too tight for him. I didn't mind the look on him.

"What were you doing?" he asked.

I don't know. What was I doing? Right. I was inspecting the crime scene. "I was — uh — watching an ant," I lied stupidly.

"An ant?" he asked skeptically while inching toward me.

I nodded. "He was carrying another ant — a soldier ant. It was interesting." *How much dumber could I possibly sound?*

Collin closed in on me until he was just a mere foot away. Then he lowered himself to the ground to sit. "Where'd it go?" He brushed the brown hair out of his eyes and inspected the grass in front of him.

His willingness to engage with me took me slightly off guard, but I managed to sit next to him and shrug. "I guess he's gone now."

We both went silent for a beat. Then Collin's words came out quickly, as if he was forcing himself to say them. "Why'd you run away from me yesterday?"

"I—" What was he talking about? I hadn't run away from him.

Oh. Realization struck. I *had* run away from him.

"I'm sorry," I managed to say. "I didn't realize it was you."

He raised his brows. "Who'd you think it was? You ran away awfully fast."

"I didn't run away *that* fast," I defended. "You could have caught up to me if you wanted to. You *were* always the fastest runner on the team."

"Why'd you quit?" His brown eyes flickered to mine before returning to stare at the grass.

"I got a job," I replied like that explained everything.

"Oh, right. At the grocery store."

The more he talked to me, the more I relaxed. It made me miss the cross country team deeply, not that we were ever close, but we were both a part of it. The familiarity left me too comfortable when I thought back to what I'd been wondering all day. It gave me the courage to speak my mind.

"Hey, Collin. I heard about your sister. I'm really sorry. What really happened to her?"

He eyed me without speaking.

"I'm sorry," I said quickly. I averted my gaze and began pulling at strands of grass. "I didn't mean to prod. It's just…I heard about it and…I guess I don't know what to think."

Collin rested his arms across his knees and nodded his head in agreement. "Join the club." He stared off into the distance for several long seconds before speaking again, his tone clipped. "She ran away."

"How do you know?" I continued to interrogate him even though I knew I should just drop it, but I couldn't get past my curiosity. "I mean, she could have—" I immediately locked my lips together when I realized I almost said she could have *died*. "Something else could have happened to her," I finished.

He shook his head. His gaze was still locked on something far away. "She left a note saying so."

My heart sank at this confirmation. "So, her secret boyfriend…"

"That's what people are saying. I don't know. I never heard her talk about a guy, but I guess if he really was secret, she wouldn't tell her little brother about it."

Silence hung in the air between us with a sort of tension that told me he didn't want to talk about it no matter how badly I craved answers.

"What are you doing up here anyway?" I asked with the intent to change the subject before mentally kicking myself. Everything that came out of my mouth at the moment had me doing that, like I was some sort of walking talking abomination that just needed to shut up.

Collin's eyes met mine, and a hint of a smile twitched at the corners of his lips. "The same thing you're doing."

Oh, God. He's looking for his sister's murderer! No, wait. That can't be it. How could he know that's what I was doing?

I forced myself to swallow. "What do you mean?"

"Running?" He said it like it was a question. "You were running, right?"

I quickly relaxed. "Yeah, right. I was. But don't you get enough of that at practice?" *Oh, my God, Kai. Just shut up.*

Collin gave a slight laugh. "Not really. I could run forever if I had the chance. That's why I don't really blame Darla for running away. I'd literally run away, too, if I thought I could."

My heart fluttered in my chest when I realized he shared one of my deepest desires. "I hear you. I want to get out of this town, too. I want to travel someday. My real dream is to go on an adventure, where I can skydive and bungee jump. I want to see and experience all the world has to offer."

"Sounds like fun. Unfortunately at this point in my life, I don't have anywhere to go, and I'm a minor. They'd drag me back home the first chance they got."

"And no one feels the same way about Darla?" I said before I could stop myself. I pressed my lips together. Clearly he didn't want to talk about her.

"What do you mean?" This time, he actually looked into my eyes.

I stared down at a leaf in front of me. "I mean, why isn't anyone out there looking for her?"

Collin shrugged before fixing his eyes on the same leaf. "Because she's eighteen and can do whatever she wants. She did the same thing last year and came home in under a week. Dad's sure that's what will happen this time."

My hands began trembling before I realized they were. I shoved them between my knees to steady them. "I heard something about that. Why'd she run away last time?" I still didn't meet his gaze, but I could feel him studying me like he wasn't sure how much to tell.

"Stupid drama," he finally answered. "She's had a rough year ever since her boyfriend broke up with her."

"Her boyfriend?"

"Shawn Cameron. As far as I knew, she wasn't involved with anyone since him, but I guess I don't know my sister as well as I thought."

Hmm…This information had me thinking, but I couldn't stop the next words that flew out of my mouth. "What kind of drama was it?"

Collin shrugged another time before shifting to cross his legs. "I don't know. It was stupid stuff like wearing the same dress as the homecoming queen. She had a sort of falling out with half of her friends last year. I don't really know. I just know she ran away that time and now she's done it again."

Except she never made it out of Amberg, I thought, which only made me want to hurl. Obviously, I couldn't say something like that to him, so instead, I changed the subject with another one of my awkwardly random blurt-out statements. "Have you ever ran away?" My pulse quickened when I asked this. Without warning, tears began to well in my eyes.

Collin scoffed. "I wish. You?"

I bit the inside of my lip and nodded nervously.

Collin shifted to rest his hands behind him on the grass. When I finally looked at him, a half-smile had formed across his face. "Do tell."

I quickly returned to staring at the yellow leaf. "I— I'd rather not."

"Come on, Kai. You can talk to me."

I twisted to look at him again. "What makes you say that?"

He straightened up again and brushed his hair from his face. "Because I find it easy to talk to you. You must feel the same about me."

What did he mean? I forced my hands deeper between my knees to ease their shakiness.

"We know each other," he encouraged. "We were once part of the same crowd."

I couldn't help but hear something in his tone that he didn't dare to say: *Before you left us.* The truth was, I *didn't* know Collin that well, yet I found myself oddly comfortable around him. Maybe it was the familiarity, or perhaps it was his calm demeanor. *Something* had me speaking to him the same way I'd talk to Savannah.

"It's silly, really," I started.

I recalled the first time I "ran away." I didn't *really* because it was in my spirit form, but something about escaping to my grandma's after hearing my parents discuss their divorce *felt* rebellious. I had told my parents I'd run away, but it was obvious that I'd been in my bed the whole time.

When my grandma died a month later, I felt the urge to get away the same way I had in my dreams. The only problem was that at that point, I still didn't really know how to control my gift, and truth be told, I wanted my parents to notice this time. They hadn't even told me about their divorce yet, and I wanted them to feel the same pain I was feeling at the time.

"Well, are you going to tell me?" Collin asked after a long silence.

I sighed. "I was twelve years old and stupid. A lot was going on in my life. My parents were going through a divorce, and my grandma had just died. She was one of my favorite people in the world."

Collin nodded like he understood.

"I just—I don't know. I wanted my parents to notice me or something. I still don't know why I did it, but I just started running. I hid under the bridge outside of town for a couple of hours until the police found me. I told my parents I'd been kidnapped. I don't know why. I guess I thought they might get back together if they thought I'd been in real trouble." I paused for a long moment. "Obviously, they didn't buy it."

Collin's laugh cut through the quietness that had settled over the bluff.

I couldn't help it when a smile twitched at my own

lips. "What's so funny?"

"You've got balls. I'll give you that. When my mom left us, all I could do was cry." Suddenly, his tone became soft. "Even when my dad told me I was being a pussy, I couldn't stop crying."

"And you're telling me this?" I couldn't imagine why he was opening up to me like this. Guys don't usually talk about crying, do they?

"I was eight. Can't a kid cry when he loses his mom?"

I blinked a few times. "I'm sorry. I didn't mean—"

"It's okay."

We both went silent again. I chewed on the dry skin covering my lower lip to keep my mouth occupied. Knowing that he'd already lost one woman in his life made my body go weak to think that he'd soon learn he'd lost another.

I broke the silence with a near whisper. "Collin, I'm so sorry."

I could have sworn I heard him sniffle, but when he looked at me, he seemed completely fine. "You have nothing to be sorry about. It's getting dark, though, and you look cold." He gestured to the goosebumps I hadn't realized had surfaced on my arms. "We should probably both be getting home."

"You're right." I rose from my seated position. I didn't know which way he would turn to head home, but I had already chosen to take the road when his voice stopped me.

"Hey, Kai?"

I turned back toward him. "Yeah?"

"It was really good talking to you again. Maybe you'll decide to join us for cross country again next year."

My mouth hung open slightly as I searched for the right words. "Collin, I—"

"I know. Your job. But there's only one season left after this one for us, and you have the rest of your life to work and travel and all that. You shouldn't let good stuff like this pass you by."

Dang, he gets pretty deep, doesn't he? "I—um—I'll try not to," I told him, but I wasn't sure how much truth there was to that statement.

7

I spent the whole walk home replaying everything Collin had said in my mind. I couldn't help but focus on the details about Darla. Obviously she had planned to run away. My initial theory came back to me. What if she didn't make it that far because her boyfriend killed her? What if that was his plan all along when he invited her to run away with him?

And how in God's name was I going to find closure?

When I returned home, I began to formulate a plan. Although I wasn't happy to see Jack, I wondered if he could help me.

I heard his voice before I saw him. When I finally caught a glimpse of him at my kitchen stove, I immediately froze. Were Jack and my mom preparing a home-cooked meal? This couldn't be happening! Mom hadn't cooked us a proper meal in what felt like ages. What was she doing cooking with Jack? Did this mean they were *together*? Oh, God, no. Please don't let that be true.

My mother's laughter died down when she noticed me. "Kai. How was your run?"

I forced myself to continue breathing. It was like my mother had been replaced with some alien look-alike who knew how to cook. "It was fine," I finally answered, although uncertainty held heavy in my tone. "What are we having?"

"Oh, this?" My mom held up flour-coated fingers and gestured to a ball of dough on the counter. "This isn't for supper. This is for Jack's family."

"Oh, don't be silly, Lisa," he interjected while rolling up a sleeve before plunging his hands into the flour.

Ew! Stop getting your germs over my family's food!

"We can leave some of the pie here for you," Jack offered.

"Pie?" I asked slowly, still frozen in place. "Mom, what's going on?" My mom rarely cooked for us. What was she doing making a homemade *pie* for Jack's family?

"Oh, stop looking at me like I'm an alien who replaced your mother," she joked far too cheerfully.

Oh, my God. How did she know that's what I was thinking? Maybe she is an alien!

"I'm just teaching Jack some cooking tricks so he can cook for his family this Thanksgiving. It's his first time hosting."

"Okay," I said like I totally understood, but I didn't. Why was it that Mom never had time to teach me how to cook?

I quietly slunk off to my bedroom and returned to the living room with my math homework. I wasn't really paying attention to it. I couldn't exactly concentrate when Braden refused to turn down the noise on his video game. I gritted my teeth and waited until my mom and Jack put the pie in the oven. Then I spoke.

"Jack?"

"Officer Delaney," he corrected while drying his hands.

"Right. Officer Delaney. Can I talk to you?"

"Sure. What about?"

My mother seemed to be paying no attention while she cleaned up their cooking mess.

"Can I talk to you in private?" I led him onto the porch and leaned against the railing without talking for several long minutes. Here it was. This was my chance to hand off Darla's death to someone else, to lift this weight from my shoulders and find closure.

Jack cleared his throat to pull me back to the conversation we were supposed to be having.

I took a deep breath, hoping he'd take me seriously. "I heard some rumors at school today, and I just thought you should know about them since you're a police officer and all. I thought maybe you could help." I dropped my gaze to the grass below me.

Jack shifted to come closer and leaned his own elbows on the guardrail. "Kai, what is this about?"

Nerves shuttered in my body. How much could I tell him? What would he believe? What did he already know?

I licked my lips to keep them from going dry. "I heard that Darla Baxter ran away."

Jack nodded like he already knew.

Okay, here it was. I quickly searched for something else to steady myself, but the railing was the best I could do. Still, it didn't seem like enough. "And there were rumors that she may have been murdered." I spat it out before I could stop myself. This wasn't true, but at least it might spark some suspicion that would send the police looking for her.

"Whoa, Kai. That's a serious accusation. Where'd you hear that?"

I forced myself to shrug. At least it was dark enough outside and the porch light was behind me so that if I was letting myself show any dishonesty, he might not catch on. "I just heard it around."

"Well, that's just silly."

Immediately, my heart dropped in my chest. There goes the hope that he might actually believe something I said. I couldn't just stop trying, though, not when I'd already made it through the toughest part.

"What's so silly about it?" I asked. "No one has heard from her in days. Everyone's talking about this secret boyfriend she has. Who's to say he didn't lure her out of the house only to murder her? He could have made her leave a note so no one would think to look for her for a while."

The muscles in Jack's jaw tightened. "How did you know she left a note?"

I immediately bit down on my lip as if I should feel guilty. "Collin told me."

"Her brother, right?"

I nodded. "So, do you think the police will investigate?" I held my breath in anticipation.

Jack's expression instantly shot down any hope I'd had. "There's no reason to. I heard she ran away—my daughter's in your high school, remember?—but it just doesn't sound like something the police should investigate."

"What does that mean?" My tone came off harsher than I intended.

Jack sighed like there was no way to explain it to me, like I was too young to understand. I was sixteen for heaven's sake!

"She's eighteen." He said it like that should explain everything.

"And? Don't adults have rights, too?"

I half expected him to say, *Don't use that tone with me*, but he didn't.

"She's eighteen, which means she can go wherever

she wants. Why worry?"

"Um, because no one knows where she is?" Okay, I was coming off way snarkier than I meant to. How could he not see that a serious investigation was needed?

Jack shifted to face me more directly. "Isn't that the point of running away? Besides, she's done it before. We launched an investigation then, and she came running back home practically before the investigation started."

"So, you're treating her like the girl who cried wolf?"

Jack glared at me, and I knew without having to read his mind exactly what he was thinking. *No, Kai, you're the girl who cried wolf.*

"So, you're not even going to help her, to worry about her?"

"I didn't say I wasn't worried. To run away like that...you could really get yourself hurt."

You have no idea, I thought.

"But that doesn't mean there's a reason to investigate. Like I said, she's an adult who's free to go where she pleases. Besides, her family hasn't filed a missing person's report."

"That's probably because her dad thinks she's going to come running back in a week like last time. That's what Collin told me."

"And that's probably exactly what will happen."

Dang it. I just killed my entire argument.

It was clear Jack wasn't going to trust my

judgement. He really *did* think of me as the girl who cried wolf. First, I'd told my parents I'd run away when I didn't, and then I really did run away and claimed I'd been kidnapped. Even though it had happened four years ago, I was sure Jack hadn't forgot the night he dragged me home after finding me under the bridge. Clearly, I wasn't very trustworthy when I was twelve, and he still thought I was that same silly young girl.

"If an investigation is needed," Jack told me, "then we'll launch one when we have a reason to start worrying."

I could hear it in his tone. That was the end of the conversation.

Jack began to head back inside but stopped at the door and turned back to me. "Your play is next week, right?"

I didn't bother mentioning that it wasn't *my* play. I wasn't even in it. I simply nodded. "It opens on Friday."

"I'll have to check it out. I'll be there, okay?"

I couldn't bring myself to react when he turned back inside. I knew he was just saying that to leave the conversation on a high note and make me feel better, but it did nothing of the sort.

That night, I lay wide awake in bed, angrily chewing on the inside of my lip while going over everything Jack had said.

Fine, I decided. *If what you need is proof, I'll have to find it.*

I couldn't dilly-dally at the bush of death any

longer. I had to launch a full-fledged investigation of my own to put this mystery to rest and get my abilities back.

8

I didn't want to sleep that night. I was afraid to relive the frightening scene of Darla's murder again, but eventually, I couldn't fight the fatigue any longer. I fell asleep and witnessed the horror once again in my nightmares. Although I managed to get some shuteye, I couldn't pass up Savannah's latest offer for a morning coffee.

"Shawn Cameron. Shawn Cameron. Shawn Cameron." That's basically all I heard come out of Savannah's mouth the entire morning. Apparently he had called her last night, and they'd spent "hours" talking on the phone and falling in love.

"He's just trying to get in your pants, you know," I said without thinking. Okay, that was a little insensitive. I shouldn't have said that.

"Well, yeah." Savannah rolled her eyes like it was obvious, which made me feel a bit better about assuming it. "That doesn't mean we can't have some fun and fall in love along the way."

I laughed along with her, but I knew that's not how she truly felt about it. I'd been friends with her long enough to understand what she was really thinking. She knew what kind of guy Shawn was, but she'd already fixed the delusion in her mind that things would be different with her. It didn't feel right to break that illusion.

"Savannah, you'll be careful, won't you?" I asked for reassurance. Hopefully it showed her how much I cared yet respected her decisions. I just didn't want her to get hurt.

Savannah scoffed like the concept of her being reckless was ludicrous. "Of course I will. You know me."

She was right. She'd been careful with guys so far when it came to that kind of stuff—she was all talk and no action—but I couldn't help but wonder if *Shawn* would be different for *her*.

I took a sip of my coffee before clearing my throat. "I know, but that doesn't mean I know or trust Shawn."

Savannah twisted her lips at me as if she was disappointed in something I'd said. "You can at least trust that I have enough sense to take care of myself, right?" Something in her tone sounded like she was asking my permission to move forward with Shawn.

"Yeah," I answered her with a smile, even though that wasn't entirely honest.

When we reached the school after breakfast, I took a deep breath before entering the doors. I had to get more serious about my "investigation," to find the courage to talk to people about Darla. Except, as I pushed through the halls and headed toward my first period class, it seemed that talk of Darla's disappearance had been completely forgotten. The latest buzz was on some breakup between two students I didn't know well. Apparently it blew up over Facebook last night. Still, I wasn't going to back down on learning more about Darla just because no one else seemed to care.

My hands shook nervously as I approached the group of students in my first period class who had been talking about Darla yesterday. "Um, hi," I greeted to get their attention. At least they stared back at me with friendly enough faces. I shyly took an empty seat next to my classmates.

"Can we help you with something?" one of the girls, Sara, asked curiously after a long silence.

"I—yeah. This might sound odd. I didn't mean to eavesdrop"—that was a total lie—"but I heard you guys talking yesterday about Darla Baxter."

"Did she come home yet?" Sara instantly leaned in closer like I had some juicy secret to tell and she was dying to eat it up. She obviously enjoyed sticking her nose into every bit of gossip that might possibly be of interest.

"No," I stated all too confidently. "I mean, I don't know." I paused for a breath as the three of my classmates stared back at me expectantly. "I was wondering what you guys knew."

The other girl, Molly, eyed me. "You didn't know her, did you?"

I pulled back slightly. I didn't really know what the statement implied. "I knew her like anyone at school knows her." Before any of them could reply, I added, "Besides, I'm friends with her brother, and I was just worried."

Sara's eyes lit up. "What does Collin know?"

"That's the problem. He doesn't know much except that—" I broke off.

"Except that, what?" the boy, Ethan, asked.

I wondered how much they knew.

"I don't know if this information will be of any use to you," I started. Heck, I didn't even know if they already knew, but there really wasn't any harm in spilling the beans. It's not like it was a secret, and if I told them something, they might trade my insight for other information. "But if I tell you, you have to tell me everything you know. Deal?"

"Deal," Sara said with certainty, as if she'd give anything to have a piece of the latest gossip.

"Okay, well, all I know is that she left a note saying she was running away."

"Really?" I didn't think it was possible, but Sara's

eyes lit up even brighter. It was a stupid piece of gossip because it didn't change anyone's assumptions about what had happened, but it seemed to interest Sara.

I nodded. "So, what do you know?"

"I'm just repeating what I heard, so I can't confirm that it's true." Sara's voice filled with enthusiasm, and I knew her unsaid words were, *But I believe every word of it.* "I heard that she was so upset she didn't win homecoming queen that she ran away with her boyfriend after the homecoming dance. She ran away before—probably for the same stupid reason." Sara rolled her eyes when she said this. "But that time she had come home within, like, a week, so everyone thinks she'll be home by the weekend."

Disappointment washed over me. Sara had told me nothing I didn't already know. I quickly ran over everything she'd just said in my head in the silence that followed. Then something clicked.

"Wait, I heard it was a secret boyfriend. Is that right?" I asked.

All three of them nodded in unison.

"So, that means he wasn't at the homecoming dance with her?"

They all exchanged glances, as if no one had wondered that on their own.

Sara furrowed her brow. "No, I guess not. I was there—and at the after party. I didn't see her with anyone. Actually, come to think of it, I didn't even see her at the after party."

"Yeah," Molly agreed, speaking slowly. "I'm pretty sure that when they tried to get a picture of the homecoming court at the party, she was one of the people who had already left. If she was at the party at all, she didn't stay all night."

Whatever the reason she left, I already knew she hadn't been there.

"No one knows this guy's name?" I asked.

They all shook their heads cluelessly.

"Thanks, guys," I said before returning to my seat just before class began.

I couldn't manage to pay attention to the board today. Something about the mystery boyfriend—who I suspected of murder—just didn't fit. How many girls went to the homecoming dance without a date? Well, besides Savannah. The difference was that Savannah didn't have a love interest, at least not at the time. What was it about this guy that Darla had to keep him such a secret? Maybe it was because Darla already knew he was dangerous.

* * *

I headed to the auditorium with my head down and my backpack slung over my shoulder. I had wondered about Darla's boyfriend all day. I'd considered asking Collin about him when I saw him in the library during my eighth hour study period, but I couldn't work up the guts to talk to him. Without any input from him, I'd come up with several theories, all of which I had no reason to believe, not even inspired by a whisper from one of my gossipy classmates. Maybe her boyfriend was a serial killer who preyed on young girls he met on the Internet. Maybe Darla had been pregnant and her boyfriend killed her because he was furious and didn't want the baby. Maybe he was married and Darla had threatened to come clean about their affair and he couldn't let his wife find out. All of it was morbid, all of it ridiculous.

I pushed through the doors of the auditorium and shook off any new silly theories. We were almost finished painting the set, but Lindsay had asked me to help her sew a few buttons on a broken costume today. I was so not looking forward to that—I didn't really know how to sew—but the poor girl seemed so busy, so I couldn't refuse.

I climbed the steps to the stage and quickly found my way to the back in search of Lindsay and her buttons. I passed a row of costumes hanging on a rack, but I didn't know which one needed the touch-ups, so I continued my search. When I couldn't find Lindsay there, I headed down the stairs toward the dressing rooms.

I immediately noticed two familiar faces engaged in a heated conversation. Tiana King had Shawn Cameron practically cowering against the hallway wall. I quickly retreated back up the stairs before they saw me. I pressed my back to the cold concrete. Something about the look in their eyes told me this was a private conversation.

"What are you doing with her anyway?" Tiana asked in a harsh whisper.

"I like her," Shawn hissed back. "Honest to God."

I tilted my head to make sure I was hearing them right. Who were they talking about?

"You better not let your penis cloud your judgement." Tiana said it like it was a threat.

"I won't. Can I please go now? I'd like to see my *girlfriend.*"

"Just don't forget that *I own you.*"

What the heck was going on? What was Shawn even doing at play practice?

Footsteps clicked against the tile floor, and I quickly realized they were headed my way. I tip-toed back up the stairs as fast as I could and snuck backstage away from Tiana and Shawn.

What could Tiana mean by "I own you"? Maybe she had eyes for Shawn and now that Darla was gone, she thought she could swoop in and take him. But what about the girlfriend he mentioned? Wait...they couldn't be talking about—

"Savannah," I greeted before practically ramming into her.

"Hey, Lindsay is looking for you. She says something about buttons and costumes."

I nodded. "I was looking for her, too. Hey, are you and Shawn calling each other boyfriend and girlfriend yet?"

A grin formed across Savannah's face. "Yeah, I guess so."

"Okay, well—"

"Kai, there you are!" Lindsay's voice interrupted.

"I'll talk to you later," I told Savannah in a near whisper just as I heard Shawn approach from behind me.

"Hey, babe," he greeted his *girlfriend* while I followed after Lindsay.

I quickly glanced back at Savannah, who was shooting me a wide smile. Just as I rounded the corner, I witnessed Shawn pull something small out of his pocket.

* * *

"Kai." Savannah's voice sounded from behind me as I lazily pulled at my split ends while leaning against the grocery store register.

I quickly straightened up. "Savannah? What are you doing here? You never visit me at work."

She rushed toward me in excitement. "I didn't have a chance to talk to you before you left rehearsal. You'll never guess what happened!" Before I had a chance to provide my input, she was already shoving a silver charm in front of my face. It swung back and forth in her hand.

"Oh, my God. Did Shawn give you that?" I leaned in to inspect the rhinestone heart. So I guess this really did make them official.

"Isn't he so sweet?" she raved.

I pulled away and returned to leaning against the counter. "That's why he was at practice earlier?"

Savannah nodded proudly. "It's the only chance he got today to talk to me. He even sat in the audience and watched me practice."

"Mr. Spears was okay with that?"

"Oh, I told him he was my boyfriend. It was no problem."

"So, you two are getting serious, then?"

Savannah rolled her eyes. "Please. We only just got together. I don't give it up that easily."

"I would hope not!"

"Don't worry," she said with a shy smile.

I watched as she balled the necklace into her fist. "You're a lucky girl," I told her with little enthusiasm to my voice.

Savannah shook her body as if shaking off nerves. "I'm just—I'm so ecstatic right now. I couldn't help but tell you as soon as practice was over."

"About practice...Savannah, I heard something earlier."

Exaggerated curiosity settled over her face. "What do you mean?"

"I don't know, to be honest. It was weird. I heard Tiana and Shawn talking. She said something about *owning* him. You don't think that...I mean, you don't think you have competition, do you?"

"What? With Tiana? No way. I mean, they dated for

a while—"

"Really?"

"Yeah, you didn't know that? It was a long time ago, like last school year."

I laughed a little. "That's not that long ago." I paused for a second. "Wait. I thought he was dating Darla last school year."

"How do you not keep up with this kind of stuff? Those two broke up last year, and then Tiana and Shawn started dating. It only lasted for two months or so."

I mulled over Savannah's words for a moment. My theory about Tiana wanting Shawn because Darla was gone didn't make sense since she'd already dated him. Then something else clicked. That must be why Tiana and Darla weren't friends anymore like Tiana had told me, because Tiana had stolen Shawn from her. That would also explain the "fallout" Collin had told me about with Darla and her friends. Except…what if Tiana still wanted to be with Shawn? That thought made me worry about Savannah.

"You don't think she has eyes for him still, do you?" I asked warily. "I mean, maybe she's jealous."

"I appreciate you telling me this, but Shawn has told me that they're just friends. Dating didn't work out with her because they'd been friends forever. Besides, it's not like anything bad happened to any of the other girls he dated since her."

That eased my worry about Tiana slightly, but it didn't make me feel any better about Shawn. "Well, I hope he's as good of a guy as you say he is. I don't want you to get hurt."

"Don't worry. I'll let you get back to work. I just wanted to show you the necklace!"

Savannah left the grocery store with a spring to her step I hadn't noticed before. She was obviously happy with Shawn, but I worried about my best friend's well-being.

9

When I arrived home, I flung on the closest running gear I could find and threw my hair up into a ponytail. Today, I found myself headed straight toward the bluff, bypassing most of the houses and the creepy cemetery on the way. I didn't know what I expected to do up there. It's not like I would find anything.

I slowed as I reached the clearing. I had some time before the last few rays of sunlight faded, and though I knew it was useless, I pushed through the trees anyway in search of some sort of *clue*. Stray red leaves had me spotting blood where there wasn't any. Upturned patches of brush made me wonder if this was the way the killer—Darla's boyfriend or whoever he was—dragged her. I was no tracker, but the patches of displaced leaves looked awfully similar to the ones I was leaving behind. They must have just been from people like me walking off the trails.

Eventually, I stumbled across one of the walking trails. Realizing how useless my search was, I picked up the trail and headed back toward the parking lot, ready to ditch the bluff altogether and give up on my search for Darla.

What does it matter anyway? I thought. *It's not like I can save her. She's already gone.* Besides, nothing I'd done up to this point had put me any closer on my search for justice. If anything, I'd only discouraged Jack from looking for her because he didn't trust me. I was ready to give up, but if I did, that meant I may never be able to astral travel again. I'd have to witness Darla's death again and again every night for the rest of my life. And what about the killer? If her boyfriend really *was* a serial killer or something, he might find another victim. Yet, what more could I do?

I couldn't help but pass by the bush of death on my way back home since it was situated next to the parking lot. I slowed as I neared it, taking one last good look around. That's when I spotted it.

There were lots of rocks around—after all, the road and parking lot were gravel—but one larger rock stuck out to me lying in the grass ten yards or so from the bush of death. It was the right size...Could it be?

I inched closer to it, my heart hammering. *Could this be the murder weapon?* Just as I leaned down to grab it, a voice cut through the silence.

"Kai?"

I sprang up immediately and locked my hands behind my back like I'd been caught doing something wrong. I relaxed when I noticed it was only Collin. "Collin. Hi."

"How is it that I always find you right here?"

I bit my lip nervously. I couldn't answer with, *Because it's where I saw your sister get murdered and I'm looking for clues.* Now that I was giving up, I guess that wasn't so much the truth anymore. "It's where I take a break. It's the halfway point on my run." I was surprised at how even my voice sounded, like I *didn't* have anything to hide from him.

Collin nodded like he understood. "What's that?" He sank to the ground and crossed his legs on the grass *right in front of the bush of death.*

I shifted in front of the rock. "What's what?" I put on my best innocent face.

"That rock." He pointed.

I glanced behind me like I had no idea what he was talking about, but I'd already been caught. "Oh, that. Nothing. I — uh — just saw it and thought it looked cool. Now that I'm up close, it's not as cool as I thought."

"Oh? Can I see it?" Collin held out his hand expectantly.

"It's not that cool," I insisted. I hadn't truly had a chance to inspect it. What if his sister's blood was on it?

"Come on. I want to see it."

I couldn't deny his insistence. I turned to swoop up

the rock and quickly flipped it over in my hands. No sign of blood. My racing heart slowed.

He shrugged as he studied it. "It is a kind of cool rock."

I sat beside him, careful to keep a generous distance from the bush of death. Several minutes passed without either of us saying anything. In the silence, I noticed how dark it was getting. Collin continued to flip the rock around in his hands, and although it truly wasn't an interesting rock, he seemed oddly interested in it. I suspected that was because it gave him something to occupy his hands and his gaze. As he inspected the rock, I subtly examined his face. His lips were turned down, and his brows were pulled together tightly. Something was bothering him, but I wasn't sure he wanted to talk about it. My own face heated the more I stared at him, and *that* bothered me.

I was just about to break the silence and tell him I should be getting home when I heard something else entirely come out of my mouth. "Is something bothering you?"

Collin's demeanor didn't change for the next few seconds, and I was sure he hadn't hear me. *Okay, time to say goodbye*, I thought, only before I could, he spoke up. It was like he had anticipated I was ready to leave but didn't want to be alone.

"Yeah, something's bothering me."

"Oh? Do you want to talk about it?"

Silence filled the space for a moment before he

finally decided to speak again. "I just don't get my sister. It's worrying me. I mean, Darla hasn't dated a lot—actually, at all—since Shawn, so how can she have this boyfriend no one seems to know anything about?"

The question was rhetorical, but I answered anyway. "Maybe that's why she kept him secret. Maybe she was still hurt about her breakup with Shawn and thought she needed someone to comfort her but wasn't confident in their relationship or something." I could hardly believe that insight came out of my own mouth. It *was* a good theory.

Collin shrugged. "I guess that makes sense, but why hasn't she come home yet? She hasn't called or anything, and when I tried to call her, it went straight to voicemail. Last time she ran away, it was like we barely had a chance to worry before she was back."

"I thought she had been gone for a week last time."

Collin eyed me. "Who told you that?"

My body tensed for some unknown reason. "No one. I just heard it around."

Collin fixed his eyes back on the rock he was rolling between his hands. "It was more like four days."

We both fell silent again before his statement sank in and I managed to speak. "Hasn't it only been four days?" I mentally kicked myself. What was I doing giving him hope when I knew there wasn't any?

Collin paused as if counting the days in his head. "I guess you're right. It feels like a lot longer. So, we should expect her home tonight, then?"

Oh, no. I couldn't give him *that* kind of hope. "You never know. What if she really likes this guy and is gone longer?" *Dang it. There I go again pretending like she's going to make it home when I know she isn't.*

"I'd like to know who this guy *is*. He seems awfully suspicious. " Collin gritted his teeth.

That was a good point. Maybe I'd been focusing on the wrong things in my investigation. If I couldn't find evidence at the crime scene, then maybe I could help by finding out who this guy she ran off with was. If he was dangerous, maybe the police would take her run away more seriously and treat it like a kidnapping. The problem was that no one seemed to know a darn thing about him. How would *I* learn more about him?

"You're sure she ran away with him?" I don't know where the question came from, but I needed the reassurance to make sure this guy was the murderer.

"Well, if she didn't run away with him, then what happened to her?" Collin asked the question like I would know the answer. "She left her car at home. It only makes sense that he picked her up and they took off together. And her note mentioned him."

He made a lot of sense.

"You really seem to care about your sister," I said to fill the silence.

His soft brown eyes met my gaze, sending my heart fluttering. "You wouldn't think that if you had talked to me last week. It's like when she's gone, I realize how much I miss her, but when she's around, all we do is fight."

"I think I get what you mean," I told him, even though I'd never lost Braden. "I have a younger brother. We fight all the time, but I would never wish it upon him to disappear the way Darla did."

The way Darla did. The words echoed in my mind, sending a shiver down my spine. No, as much as I disliked my brother, I wouldn't wish death upon him.

I thought I saw tears rise to Collin's eyes, which made me immediately regret what I'd just said. Sorrow filled my soul, and all I wanted to do was hug Collin and tell him everything would be alright, even though that was a complete lie. He'd never get his sister back.

"Doesn't that suck?" he asked without looking at me.

"What do you mean?"

"Families are the worst, but you can't help but love them to death because they're your family. It seems all my dad and I do is fight. He's always yelling, but I mean, he'll always be my dad. Even with how hard things have been this week, I'll always love him."

I spoke slowly, not sure if I had Collin's complete trust. "Hard, as in, because Darla is gone?"

He shifted until he was facing me. "My dad may say he doesn't care about what Darla does with her life, but I can tell he's worried, too. He's really mad at Darla for running away, but he's been taking it out on me, you know?"

What did he mean by that? I'd never met his dad.

Was he violent? Thankfully, Collin clarified.

"It's stupid stuff like yelling at me to do my chores *while I'm doing them* or flipping out because the neighbor's leaves blew into our yard — like they can help that. Honestly, the guy is a total dick, but I also realize he's just worried about her."

Dang, Collin must be pretty level-headed to recognize that, I thought. *Even I don't understand the madness that is my family.*

"So, why doesn't he report her missing?" I asked.

Collin shrugged. "I don't know if she's *technically* missing. I just hope she's happy wherever she ran off to."

I swallowed the lump in my throat, but my voice still came out sounding small. "Do you think something bad could have happened to her?"

Collin didn't answer, and it didn't feel right to prod. Finally, he spoke. "It's getting dark. We should both be getting home."

He pulled himself up from the ground, but before he made it all the way, I grabbed for his wrist. I don't know why I did it. I don't even remember thinking about doing it. All I knew was that one moment we were sitting on the ground together and the next I was clutching him. His soft skin warmed my chilly fingers. Collin straightened up and stared down at me expectantly. I could sense something behind his eyes, something I couldn't quite pinpoint but had the sudden urge to protect him from.

"Let me walk you home," I heard myself say.

For the first time all night, I watched a smile creep across Collin's face. "I'd like that."

Just as I was about to release his wrist, Collin's own hand came to grip my forearm, and he pulled me up from the ground. I couldn't explain the desire that overcame me to slip my fingers through his, but I didn't act on it. Instead, I let my arm fall to my side as we made our way down the bluff together. I had to force myself to keep it there.

Neither of us spoke. It was like we were both too afraid to say anything. When we reached the bottom of the bluff, Collin hurried his pace, and I followed along until we were jogging side by side. A hint of a smile touched his lips, and he glanced at me sideways. I wasn't sure what he was trying to communicate with his expression, but I guessed he was thrilled to have a running partner, just like I was.

We had to pass the cemetery, the one that had started giving me the creeps as Halloween approached. I noticed Collin wasn't too keen on the sight of grave markers either since he sped up as we passed it. Soon, we reached a more populous part of town where street lamps lit our route.

I kept up with Collin easily, and I suspected he had chosen his pace for my benefit. After all, he had always been a faster runner than me. It didn't matter the pace, though. Just feeling my feet move under me was excitement enough. My feet grew happier the more we pushed along, and my legs cheered in joy at the sensation of the workout. Something about it all felt more satisfying with Collin beside me. The cold air didn't even register on my skin as we ran.

All too soon, we slowed, and Collin stopped in front of a house I recognized though didn't know was his. I'd been paying so much attention to how much I loved running that I didn't really realize where we were going. The houses on this block seemed elaborate to me, much in contrast to my home. They were generously spaced, giving each homeowner plenty of land for a backyard pool. At least, I suspected something like that lay behind the two-story brick beauty. The lawn was gorgeously landscaped and had been well maintained. We hadn't even raked our leaves this year, which made our house look like a total dump in comparison. I imagined the interior was even more handsome than the lawn, but I knew asking to go inside would be rude. I already felt like I'd overstepped some lines with Collin by asking so many questions about Darla.

Collin turned to me on the sidewalk and ran his fingers through his hair. "Uh — thanks for walking me home."

"It wasn't much of a walk," I teased. My pulsing heart rate served as a reminder of our run.

Collin let out a puff of air that sounded like a laugh. "Well, if you're like me, you'd rather run than walk. Was I correct in assuming that?"

I didn't even have to think about it. I'd always

enjoyed running. There was just something about it that filled me with a sense of happiness and pride each time I completed a workout. "You were right."

"I'll see you tomorrow at school?" He said it like it was a question, like he was hoping we'd meet up at some point.

Did that mean he enjoyed spending time with me? My heart fluttered at the thought. Before I could answer, a deep voice cut through the momentary silence.

"Collin!"

We both jerked our eyes toward the door where the voice had come from. A tall man with dark hair stood on the steps and held the door open. The front light on the house illuminated his features. He looked a lot like Collin, except his jaw was squarer and his eyes were filled with darker emotions. I had no doubt this was the "dick" father Collin had told me about.

"Get your ass in here, boy!" he shouted across the lawn.

My eyes widened. Did he really just talk like that? An uncomfortable sensation settled over me.

"Sorry, I have to go," Collin apologized quietly to me. "Thanks for keeping me company."

Then he ran off toward the door before I could say another word. Although I didn't want to part with him yet, I turned toward home. Unfortunately, that didn't keep me from overhearing his father's next words.

"What the hell did I tell you? No more running after dark. And who's the girl you're with?"

The door fell closed behind both of them before I caught an answer. I rushed off toward the other side of town led only by the light from the streetlamps.

10

I audibly groaned when I entered my house and saw Jack sitting at my kitchen table. He was leaning over my mother's shoulder—their faces far too close if you ask me—and staring at scattered pieces of paper lying in front of them.

I pressed my hands to my temples in hopes of warding off the frustration. No such luck. It didn't appear as if they noticed my entrance, and I didn't announce it, either. I slipped off my tattered old running shoes and then hurried to my room. I didn't even bother scouring for a meal. Besides, I wasn't hungry. At least, I didn't want to be if Jack was in my kitchen.

I didn't know what it was about Jack, but just the sight of the guy put me in a state of pure irritation. Tonight, it wasn't just about him, though. The way

Collin's dad swore at him had me angry for reasons I couldn't quite pinpoint. I guess I felt sorry for Collin. As much as I was constantly annoyed with my family, we never swore at each other. I couldn't imagine being in Collin's world right now — his mother and sister gone and his father taking it all out on him. A pounding in my head flared just thinking about it.

I grabbed the towel that hung off the back of my desk chair. In the bathroom, I stripped off my running clothes, brushed out my hair, and climbed into the shower, not once taking my mind off Collin and his father. The hot water hit me with a sense of comfort, but it wasn't strong enough a stimulation tonight to ease the tension forming in my face and shoulders. I sank down to sit in the tub without even washing myself first. All I could do was take in the heat and think about Collin.

Why did I continue to give him hope tonight? I questioned myself. *Why didn't I just tell him the truth?*

Honestly, the truth didn't make any sense. I knew Darla had died, but how did that knowledge help anything? I didn't know what had happened afterward. Heck, I didn't even know who the guy who'd hurt her was.

That thought took me through a series of serious speculations. Who was her secret boyfriend? Why would she run away with him if she knew he was dangerous? What if he wasn't dangerous? I mean, how could a guy you love and trust turn around and kill you? That's the type of guy you should be running *from*, not *toward.*

To say it hit me like a ton of bricks would be an understatement. No, the realization that followed was much more intense.

Maybe she was *running from her killer.*

A knock rattled the bathroom door. "Hurry up! I have to take a massive dump," Braden's voice sounded from behind it.

I sprang up in the shower, suddenly realizing how long I'd been sitting under the cascade of water. "Well, you're going to have to wait!" I shouted back. Why anyone would design a house with only one bathroom, I'll never know.

I quickly washed and rinsed down to satisfy my brother and then hurried back into my room, although not before exchanging a few unpleasantries with him.

After drying and brushing my hair, I turned to the only thing I could think of to calm me down: my dream books. I pulled the oldest one from my bookcase and settled into bed with it. Memories of the places I'd been when I first started traveling flooded my mind as I turned the pages and examined the photographs. I'd started with some of the more popular destinations: the Eiffel Tower, the Leaning Tower of Pisa, and the Pyramids of Giza to name a few.

I couldn't help but think that I was glad I took the chance to visit these places when I could. My prior frustrations about my gift suddenly seemed silly. Why didn't I just appreciate it while I had it instead of complaining about its limitations? I guess I got what was coming to me. Karma's a bitch, they say, right? Except that bad things still happened to good people, like Darla.

That ill sensation in my gut returned. *Darla*. Could my latest theory be true? Was it even right to think about? What if Darla hadn't been running toward her boyfriend but was running away from her father? Could that make her father dangerous? I mean, I'd seen the guy yell at his own son over nothing. The guy was clearly a jerk, but was he capable of murder, and murdering his own daughter nonetheless?

The more I thought about it, the more it made sense in my head. Here's how I theorized it went down: Darla hated her father and found a guy who she felt comfortable with, who would keep her safe. She probably met him on the Internet or something and kept him a secret so her dad wouldn't find out. The only problem was that — as Collin and I talked about earlier — she still had a special place in her heart for her family, and she left a note to keep them from worrying or searching for her. But before she could make it out of town, her dad found the note and followed her to the bluff — maybe where she was meeting her boyfriend? I didn't have that part figured out yet — and killed her out of rage.

I pondered this theory longer, not sure if it even made sense. Was that motive enough to kill? More importantly, if Darla's father killed her, was Collin safe?

And what could I possibly do about it?

Nothing. That's the answer that came to mind. I couldn't go to the police with a *speculation*, and it's not like they'd believe a word I said anyway. Heaven knows that talking to Jack was a useless cause. Collin and *I* could run away together, but how far would we get before people found out we were minors and sent us right back to our crappy homes?

Stop feeling sorry for yourself! I buried my face in my pillow, but it did nothing to ease the tension forming in my head. I hated myself right now for thinking such things. Why would I want to run away from my family? I mean, sure, we don't exactly get along, but it's not like anyone was abusing me or anything. Besides, I didn't have a ton of money to run away with thanks to Mom constantly borrowing my savings and "promising" to pay me back. Fat chance of that!

Sure, I wanted to experience the world, but running away didn't make any sense. It may only get me killed the way it had with Darla.

An image of her lifeless eyes played through my mind again. The poor girl. *That's* who I should be feeling sorry for, not myself. I laid my book aside on the floor next to my bed, not wanting to escape the comfort of my covers. What good was dreaming of traveling when I couldn't literally do that anymore? Besides, my travels didn't need my attention. Darla deserved my full attention. When I couldn't bring her killer to justice, allowing her my thoughts and prayers was the least I could do.

I curled my legs to my chest as I rested my head on my pillow. A single tear fell down my cheek before I drifted off and dreamt of Darla's death for the fourth night.

11

Savannah invited me to Amberg Hamburg again the next morning. It felt that this morning coffee run thing was going to become a daily habit. I agreed to meet her there, but I'd managed to get enough sleep that I didn't think I needed the coffee. I saved my cash and came only to keep Savannah company.

"Hey, girlie," she greeted when I found my seat across from her. She was already clutching onto a steaming cup of coffee and had left the top off to help it cool down. A light brown color filled the cup thanks to the mounds of creamer and sugar she'd dumped in it—just the way I liked it, too.

I almost considered buying some when the tasty aroma hit my nose, but I reminded myself that every penny toward my big adventure counted.

"Hi, Savannah. How have you been?"

The smile that settled over her face told me she'd been in a pure state of joy the last few days. "Is that even a real question?" she teased. "It's great! Too bad I couldn't wear his necklace today." She touched a hand to her chest like she was already missing the charm she'd never worn. "It needs a new clasp, and my mom didn't have a good one for it. She's going to pick one up for me when she can and then fix it. She's practically as happy as I am."

"Well, yeah. Who wouldn't be excited about their daughter dating one of the most popular guys in school?" I intended the words to be serious, but they came out sounding more sarcastic than anything. Savannah didn't seem to notice.

She leaned forward in her seat, her eyes locked on me. "Are you busy tomorrow night?"

I didn't know why she was asking, but I pondered the question for a few seconds. Besides work, which really didn't keep me out late, I didn't have anything to do—unless my run counted, which may or may not result in an unofficial date with Collin.

Did I really just think of it that way? Just because Collin and I crossed paths on our jogs didn't mean anything special. Besides, we'd only started running into each other. *Why is that?* I wondered. It's not like he *intentionally* stumbled across me every night. So I guess the answer was no, I didn't have any plans.

"Besides work, I'm not busy," I answered. "What

were you thinking?"

Savannah was really good at suggesting things to do over the weekend. Most of the time, I accepted her offers unless it was during work hours or was the polar opposite of my style, like the homecoming dance.

"Want to hang out for a good old-fashioned sleepover?" she asked casually.

Now *that* was my style. Savannah's house was the best. They even had a trampoline.

"I'd love to!" I answered almost too quickly.

"Awesome." After a short silence, Savannah spoke again. "So, Shawn called me again last night. He says he wants to take me out Saturday night."

"That should be fun." I smiled. If only I had a guy who would take me out...

Savannah wiggled her eyebrows at me.

"Well, don't have *that* much fun," I joked.

After a sip of her coffee, her expression reverted to normal. "Don't worry about that. But seriously, I have been dying to spend more time with him. Yay for parents and their curfews!" Sarcasm held thick in her voice.

"Speaking of curfews, can I tell you something?" I glanced around and lowered my voice. After Savannah nodded, I continued. "So, on my evening jogs, I've run into Collin Baxter a couple of times."

"Ooh." Savannah wiggled her eyebrows for a second time.

"Oh, stop," I insisted, swatting at her playfully. "It's

not like that. It's just a coincidence. Our running routes cross, and we've talked a couple of times."

"Why didn't you tell me?" she asked like she was hurt.

"Because there's nothing special to tell." Honestly, most of our conversations were centered on Darla, and I hadn't had the guts to open up to Savannah about that yet. I wished I could, but I still didn't know how to explain it all. At this point, I wasn't sure it mattered since I'd pretty much resolved to giving up. The good news was that I could open up to her about some things, and having someone to talk to took a bit of the weight off my shoulders.

I drew in a deep breath. "The thing is that I met his dad. His dad was…harsh."

Savannah leaned in curiously.

"He yelled at him for staying out past dark, which is ridiculous because it gets dark pretty early now. Weird curfew, right?"

Savannah nodded in agreement.

"It wasn't just that, though," I complained, the tension in my shoulders relieving slightly. "He swore at him. Have your parents ever swore at you?"

Savannah furrowed her brow. "Of course not."

"Right? The guy seemed like a dick."

"Sounds like it." She sipped at her coffee again.

I continued to complain quietly, and I appreciated how attentively Savannah listened. When I was done, I felt more relaxed than I had all week. Before Savannah could rise to throw out her now empty cup, I stopped her.

"Hey."

"Yeah?" She looked at me expectantly.

"You won't tell anyone about this, will you?" For some reason, I felt the need to protect Collin. I knew Savannah was eager for hot gossip as much as the next girl, but she was more loyal than she was gossipy.

She tilted her head sympathetically. "Of course not. I'm your best friend, and it was clearly bothering you, but Collin deserves his privacy, too."

I smiled. I knew I wouldn't regret talking to Savannah, but there was only so much I could tell her. Even as good of a friend as she was, she'd send me straight to the psychiatric ward if I told her about my gift.

"So, what do you want to do tomorrow night?" I asked, leading us back to casual conversation.

Savannah bounced up and headed to the trash while I trailed behind her. "I was thinking the trampoline?"

I rolled my eyes. "Well, that's a given."

We both laughed.

* * *

I spotted Collin when I entered the school. His eyes didn't catch mine, but much of the tension I'd let go of earlier came rushing back. I wanted to give up on all of this because there was nothing I could do, but if Collin's dad really was guilty, how could I let Collin continue living with him? What if Collin was in danger? Maybe I could find a way to warn him…

I still hadn't come up with a way to confront the issue by lunch time. I mean, what was I supposed to do? I couldn't outright tell him that I suspected his dad was a murderer. For all Collin knew, his sister was still out there.

Savannah was chatty enough to take my mind off it for a minute. "Shawn passed by my locker between second and third period. Did you see?" she raved.

I hadn't. My second and third period classes were across the hall from each other, so I didn't go back to my locker between them.

Before I could answer, she continued while we strolled to the lunchroom. "It was like a scene straight from a high school chick flick."

I could practically see the scene as if I'd witnessed it. In my mind, Savannah's back was pressed against the locker while she twisted a strand of blue-tipped hair around her finger and stared dreamily into Shawn's eyes, his body too close for my liking.

"And then he *kissed* me!" Savannah gushed. "Right there in the middle of the hall."

I audibly gasped. "Did you get in trouble?"

"None of the teachers saw."

"Sounds romantic," I said when we reached the end of the lunch line. She was lucky to have a guy in her life.

Savannah stood on her toes, and her eyes fixed

toward the front of the line. "So, what's for lunch?"

"I think it's spaghetti, isn't it?"

She scrunched her face up. "Yuck. The school's spaghetti sucks."

"I second that," a deep voice from behind me agreed.

I whirled around, startled to find Collin Baxter standing there. Stupidly, the first thing that came out of my mouth was, "Don't you normally go off campus for lunch?"

He didn't seem taken aback by my question or wonder how I'd noticed—I guess I paid enough attention. Instead, he simply agreed with me. "I do. Have you seen what this school serves? I just wanted to see if they were having anything good, and clearly they're not. Want to go off campus?"

My jaw nearly dropped to the floor. He was asking me out to eat? Like, on a date?

"Sounds tasty," Savannah answered before I could.

Oh, right. He was inviting both of us, not just me.

"Where do you go?" I asked.

"Best place in town." He smiled.

Five minutes later, we were standing in line at Amberg Hamburg. I managed to give up a few of my precious dollars for a hamburger and smoothie. The place was packed thanks to being the only decent place in town to eat—and no doubt thanks in part to spaghetti day. We made our way outside, where there were plenty of empty tables to choose from. Despite the nice weather, most students had stayed indoors for lunch.

"Feels like a good day for a run," Collin said while taking a deep breath of fresh air.

I agreed before eagerly biting into my burger.

"Speaking of running," Savannah started, "what happened to your sister running away?"

"Savannah," I practically choked, scolding her. Only a second later did I realize that I'd approached the subject in pretty much the same manner.

"No, it's okay," Collin assured me. "A lot of people have been asking me that. The honest truth is that I don't really know. I didn't really want to talk about it at first, which is why everyone thought she was out sick on Monday. Then a couple of her friends asked me where she was. Honestly, I thought they'd know something I didn't, but she didn't even tell them she was leaving. I told them what I knew, which wasn't much."

I swallowed hard without fully chewing my food. It did nothing to relieve the lump forming in my throat. This had gone on too long. Collin deserved to know, didn't he? If he didn't know, then he wouldn't find the closure he needed, either, and he'd always wonder what happened to his sister. What was worse was that he may be living with a murderer, and if his dad could so easily kill his own daughter, what would stop him from killing his son if he stepped out of line? I couldn't let that happen to him, not if I could prevent it.

Only, what could I say? Silly explanations had been swimming around in my head all day, but none of them were remotely believable. *No, I can't.* I could almost hear my heart pounding as I contemplated this.

"I'm sorry to hear that," Savannah told him. "If you don't know what happened, then who does?"

Logic told me I couldn't tell him, and I was sure I'd decided for about the fifteenth time that day that it just wasn't going to happen, which was why I was just about as shocked as anyone when I heard the next words come out of my mouth.

"I do."

12

Savannah spat her soda across the table the same moment Collin stopped chewing. Her eyes nearly bulged out of her head. "What do you mean you know what happened to her?" Savannah asked.

I stared down at my burger guiltily like I'd done something wrong. Maybe I had. I'd kept it from Collin long enough, and now I was about to chicken out because I had no way to explain it all.

"I'm sorry. I didn't mean that."

"Well, what did you mean?" Collin asked slowly but curiously.

"I—" I looked between both of them. They were expecting an answer, and I didn't know what to give them. I hadn't even planned to say anything.

"Kai." Savannah eyed me seriously from across the

table. "What did you hear?"

Wait. She thought I knew what happened to Darla because of gossip? It was a simple excuse that wouldn't result in me being shipped off to the mental institution. I could do this. I could play along with her assumption.

I glanced around quickly, but the only other group of students were seated at the farthest table away while the rest were packed inside. I lowered my voice anyway. "I just heard something, okay? I don't know if it's true." My stomach churned in response to lying to them, but I didn't see the alternative. Tell them I saw it first-hand while outside my own body? They would never believe that, and I'd end up ten paces back from where I started. At least right now they both trusted me.

Collin shifted in his seat. "What did you hear?"

I took a deep breath, stalling to formulate the lie I knew I needed to tell them. "I was in the bathroom earlier when I heard these two girls come in. They didn't know I was there, and they started talking about how they heard something about what happened to her. The one told the other that it was secret, that not a lot of people knew." I glanced at both of them nervously. They were eating it up while I was stunned that my story sounded so believable. My English teachers had always told me I had a way with stories. I guess that made sense considering the lies I'd made up over the years.

Savannah sipped her soda like it was any old story. "Who were they, the girls?"

I shrugged, hoping to God I could maneuver my way around this plot hole. "I have no idea. I didn't see them because I was in the stall."

"What did they say?" Collin leaned in closer with a serious expression on his face. "What happened to my sister?"

I could see it in his eyes that he was in pain and eager to know. How much more would this hurt him? I chomped down on my lip to keep the tears from coming. This was it, and I wasn't sure I wanted to do it. "You're not going to like it."

"She's my sister, Kai."

"I know." I took in a deep breath, but it did little to calm my shaking fingers. I slid them into my hoodie sleeves and shoved them between my knees. "They said...they thought..." My voice cracked as an image of Darla's murder played through my mind once more. It didn't matter how many times I saw it. It didn't make it any easier.

Collin's voice softened, and he rested a hand on my shoulder. "You can tell us."

I couldn't hide the tears welling in my eyes. He deserved to know the truth, even if I wasn't honest about how I came across the information. "They said she was dead," I finally finished in a small voice.

They both gasped in unison.

"What? How?" Savannah asked quickly.

"I didn't hear much more of the conversation," I lied. "I just heard that they thought she was murdered."

Savannah's eyes narrowed in skepticism the same time Collin's hand smacked against the table. The noise earned us a few odd glares from the students nearby.

"Collin," I said quietly. This time, I rested *my* hand on *his* shoulder.

He pressed two fingers to his eyes but remained surprisingly calm. "These girls?" he asked without lifting his head. "Do you think they were a reliable source?"

"I don't know. Like I said, I don't know who they were. I don't know how they knew, but they sounded serious."

"Why didn't you tell me?" Pain filled his voice.

I knew immediately that I'd hurt him, and I instantly regretted it, but I couldn't turn back now. I was already committed to the lie.

"I didn't get a chance until now." Another blatant lie. A tear fell down my face, partially because I hated lying to my friends like this and partially because I couldn't bear to watch Collin cry. I didn't actually see any tears, but I could tell he was grieving behind the hand he pressed to his face.

I should come clean, I thought. *About my abilities. About it all. I can't lie to them like this.* I opened my mouth to speak, only Collin beat me to it.

He raised his head. "I knew it. I mean, I knew it was more than just her running away. She would have called by now at least. Maybe not me, but at least one of her friends."

If he believed it, then I didn't really have to spill my secret, did I? I'd already accomplished my goal by letting him in on Darla's death. I didn't have to tell him about my gift.

"So, you believe it?" I asked hopefully. If he did, then maybe he could find closure. Maybe he'd be safe from his dad.

"I have to. It's the only thing that makes sense. I may not have been that close with my sister, but I *know* her. Last time she was gone…she changed afterward. I can't really explain how, but I knew she wouldn't run away again."

"Are you sure she wouldn't?" Savannah asked uncertainly. "I mean, murder? It may not even be true." She shifted toward me. "Did you hear the girls say anything else? Who did it? Where it happened?"

I shook my head. "There are theories."

"What do you mean by that?" Collin asked.

I took a deep breath. *Okay, here comes some of the truth. I can do this.* "The first theory is that her boyfriend killed her."

"The boyfriend no one has ever heard of?" Collin asked like he didn't believe there actually was one.

"Well, her note said she was running away with him, didn't it?"

Collin nodded. "Yeah, it did. Did you hear anything else?"

Then I realized I should include another important detail. "They said they heard it happened on the bluff."

Savannah gasped again. "How would they even know this stuff?"

My heart hammered against my chest. Was I coming off too unbelievable? "I have no idea," I lied again before turning to Collin. "I think you should get your dad to file a missing person's report. I think the police should investigate."

Collin went silent for a moment before answering. "I agree, but I don't know if it will happen. I tried talking to him about my suspicions, that I thought Darla would at least have contacted someone by now. He's just so mad at her for leaving that he can't see that she might be in danger."

His dad is hiding something, I thought to myself. And that was the next theory I had. I needed to tell Collin in case *he* was in danger, but before I could, we were distracted by noisy students exiting the restaurant.

"It looks like it's time to head back. We don't want to miss class," Savannah pointed out. She stood to throw out her trash.

I quickly guzzled down the rest of my smoothie and shivered as it flowed down my throat. "Collin," I stopped him before he stood.

"Yeah?" He stared at me expectantly, and something in his eyes broke my heart. It was pain, pain for his sister.

"Why are you so quick to believe in this?" Honestly, I didn't think he'd buy it, even if I was able to conjure up a semi-believable lie.

As he stood to throw away his trash next to the raised flower bed nearby, he answered. "Because I already knew something bad happened to her."

* * *

I headed off to my next class full of worry for Collin. I hadn't had a chance to divulge the second theory, the one about his dad. I'd already come this far, and I needed to warn him so he'd be safe. The problem was that I didn't see him the rest of the day. I thought I might spot him in the library like normal during my study period, but I checked every table, and he was nowhere in sight. He must have stayed in his study hall room, but we weren't in the same study hall, so I couldn't go find him to talk to him.

I settled into one of the couches by the door to the library and spread my math textbook and homework across my legs. It was so quiet that I could hear the clock ticking on the wall. Every minute or so, I gazed up toward the door, expecting Collin to walk in and find a seat beside me, but he never did.

I couldn't stop thinking about Collin as I helped Lindsay patch up another costume and then headed off to work. I considered telling Meg I was sick and asking if I could leave, but for some strange reason, it was like everyone in town decided to do their grocery shopping tonight. That probably wasn't true, but I was too stressed out to think clearly.

When I returned home after work, I quickly

changed into my running clothes and eagerly raced to the bluff. I plopped down at our usual meeting spot and huffed as my heart rate slowed. For the first time in hours, I began to relax. I sank onto my back, pointed my knees up toward the sky, and worked on controlling my breathing. The cool air felt refreshing on my hot, sweaty skin.

Collin should be here any minute. Then I can get all of this off my chest and protect him like I should have days ago.

I figured I was just misestimating the time when it seemed like forever and he still hadn't shown, but when the last bits of sunlight finally faded, I realized he wasn't coming tonight. I pushed myself up from the ground and looked around just to make sure he wasn't nearby. Closing my eyes, I listened intently, hoping to hear the crunch of leaves and his labored breathing from running up the bluff, but all I heard was the soft rustle of the wind blowing through the trees.

I sulked home and nearly cursed when I saw Jack in my kitchen again. What was he doing here? Were he and my mom seeing each other without telling me? I didn't even want to know what they were doing together. First she was cutting his hair, and then she was cooking with him, all the things she was supposed to do with me, and now he was back here again?

I escaped to the bathroom to take a shower, but it did nothing to calm me like normal. When I emerged into the hallway, the smell of pizza hit my nose. I dressed in my pajamas and headed to the kitchen, hoping Jack would be gone by now. He was.

"Thanks for supper," I told my mom when I entered the kitchen.

She and my brother were both seated at the table chewing on their pizza slices.

"You can thank me," Braden said with a smirk. "I'm the one who made it."

I almost bit back with a sarcastic, *Congratulations*, but then I realized how much Braden had been preparing food lately. Wasn't that my mom's job? I quickly grew irritated at her for making Braden do it all the time. It's not like twelve-year-olds should be in charge of feeding their families.

I offered Braden a smile after grabbing a pizza slice. "Thank you, Braden. I really appreciate it. It's nice of you to cook for us all the time." I stole a glance at my mother, hoping she would catch the edge to my tone that implied that I didn't think he should be doing all the cooking. She didn't seem to notice.

"Uh, thanks," Braden said. "Stop being so weird."

After a few bites of my pizza and an extended silence, I spoke again. "Hey, Mom. I'm going to stay the night at Savannah's tomorrow."

My mother let out a breath of air. "I wish you would ask me first."

I stopped chewing. "I did just ask you."

"No, you told me."

"What's the difference?"

"Kai," she scolded in a voice that caught me by

surprise.

My unblinking eyes shifted between her and my brother as if searching for an answer about what I did wrong.

"I'm your *mother*. I wish you would respect me like I was."

Oh, no. She did *not* just go there. If we wanted to talk about respect, let's talk about how she respected me as a daughter, always taking my money without paying me back, and suddenly dating a guy she didn't even bother to tell me about—or for that matter ask if I was comfortable with.

But I didn't say any of this. I shoved the last bite of pizza in my mouth and suddenly lost my appetite. Realizing that keeping quiet was the best thing I could do, I rose from my chair and headed back toward my room.

"Kai," she called. "Where are you going?"

"I'm done eating," I insisted.

I clicked off my light and crawled into bed too early. Images of the places I'd traveled played through my mind. I wanted to get away so badly, but daydreaming about traveling was nothing compared to lucidly dreaming about it. My astral travels felt like a whole lifetime ago, and now I wasn't sure if I would ever find the closure I needed to get them back.

I knew I was acting childish and stupid and selfish. Even at the time, I realized it, but I couldn't help it when the tears came. I entered into another night of bad dreams.

13

When I woke Friday morning, I was aware that I'd relived the night of Darla's murder again, but I'd slept better than I had the last few nights.

I walked to school on my own. I hadn't received Savannah's coffee invite this morning, so maybe it wasn't going to be a daily thing. Even as I entered the school, I couldn't shake off the feeling of living in a daze. I hardly registered conversations around me, and I didn't think I would have noticed if all of the students spontaneously disappeared.

"'Ello, sweetie," Savannah greeted in her near-perfect British accent. She took the seat across from me in the commons before class.

I snapped to attention. "What's up?"

"My mom found a clasp for me. Check it out." She

held her charm out toward me.

I played along and inspected it like it was the first time I was seeing it. "Ooh, pretty."

"I know." She smiled before slipping the necklace back under the black hoodie that matched her dark hair.

"Not as good as mine," I joked, pulling the dreamcatcher necklace away from my chest to inspect it. I had bought the necklace a couple of years ago at a flea market Savannah dragged me to. It reminded me of my gift, but now it only mocked the fact that I could no longer travel in my sleep.

"Well, yours *is* pretty," she admitted.

It was just a small metal charm the size of a quarter, but I liked it enough to continue wearing it. Plus, the silver matched pretty much every outfit I wore, including the green cardigan I'd slipped on this morning.

"Well, you're one lucky girl," I told her. "To have Shawn, I mean."

"Please," she teased. "He's the lucky one."

I couldn't help but smile at Savannah. She was definitely right about that one.

"I think I should formally meet him. After all, if he's your boyfriend, we'll be spending more time together at some point."

Savannah ran her fingers through her blue tips. "Yeah, I guess you're right. Too bad you don't have a boyfriend so we could double date."

Please don't remind me.

The bell rang just then.

"I can't wait until you come over tonight," Savannah said before we took our separate ways at our lockers.

I barely paid attention in class that day. I hoped Collin might invite Savannah and me out again for lunch, but when I made it to the lunch room, I saw him already headed out the doors.

Savannah caught me in the lunch line. "Kai, Shawn is going to take me out for lunch, okay? I'll see you later." She bounced off the in the opposite direction, radiating happiness. At least the guy seemed good for her.

Too bad she hadn't invited me along. I didn't want to intrude on their semi-date, but the problem was that without Savannah with me at lunch, I didn't really have anyone to talk to. Sure, I sat by our group of "friends," but they were more Savannah's friends than they were mine, and since I sat at the end of the table, I felt slightly left out. The upside was that I had enough on my mind to occupy my thoughts for a lifetime, so lunch seemed to pass by quickly.

When eighth hour study hall rolled around, I was relieved to find Collin sitting alone at one of the tables in the library. I sat in the chair across from him and slid my textbook onto the table in front of me.

He jumped but relaxed when he saw it was only me. Dark shadows sat beneath his eyes like he hadn't slept last night.

"Collin, are you okay?" I asked quietly since we were in the library and were supposed to keep our voices down.

He rubbed his face with one hand. "I guess I'm fine, in a sense. I mean, how good can a guy be after what you told me yesterday?"

"Collin, I—"

"It's not your fault."

After a brief silence, I spoke again. "Where were you yesterday?"

"What do you mean? When?"

"Everywhere. You weren't here in the library. You weren't at the bluff."

"Oh." He shrugged. "I stayed in my study hall room just kind of thinking. Then we had a cross country meet last night, just like every Thursday."

Right. I should have realized that.

"And then things got really stressful at home." He didn't meet my gaze when he talked about this, but he said it like he trusted me. "I tried to tell my dad what you told me—about the rumors. He wouldn't hear any of it. He said they were just rumors. I think he's just trying to see how long Darla will stay away this time, only I'm afraid she'll never come back." Collin sighed. "I told him I wanted to go down to the police station and file a missing person's report, but he's all like, 'Your sister isn't missing. She's an adult who can do whatever she wants.'" The words sounded all too familiar, like what Jack had said to me. Collin didn't speak for a long time after that.

I finally broke the silence. "Collin, I didn't mean to hurt you."

"Kai," he stopped me. "It's not your fault. I'm just glad you were honest with me."

Guilt knotted in my stomach. Did it count as being honest if I wasn't truthful about how I knew everything I told him?

"About that," I started, twisting my cardigan sleeve around in my fingers. "I have more to tell you."

His brow furrowed. "What do you mean?"

Just then, a figure plopped down onto the chair next to mine. My body gave a start, and I had to force my heart to slow when I saw it was only Savannah.

"What are you doing here?" I asked a little too harshly. "You don't have study hall this period."

"I know," she said with a quiet voice. "My team for economics is here to gather some research. I saw you guys and thought I'd join you."

"Shouldn't you be researching with them?" Collin asked.

"Nah, they're fine without me."

"Kai was just going to tell me something else she heard. Apparently she didn't get to finish her story yesterday."

Savannah's eyes lit up, instantly intrigued. They both stared at me, waiting for my confession.

Even though we were already talking in whispers, I lowered my voice even further. "Here's the thing...It's another theory, but again, you aren't going to like it."

"I can handle it," Collin assured me.

My breathing wavered. I wasn't so sure about that, but maybe since he lived with his dad, he'd know what he was capable of. "So, the one theory is that Darla's boyfriend killed her—after she ran away with him. The other is…"

Could it be? It sounded silly to say it out loud, but it made so much sense in my head.

"Collin, it's that your dad did it." I held my breath in anticipation of his reaction.

"That's stupid," he finally said.

"I know it sounds far-fetched, but it makes sense. What if he found her note and then killed her before she could get out of town? What if he was that mad at her?"

"Kai, listen to what you're saying. Sure, my dad is pissed at Darla, but he's not a killer."

"Then why won't he file a missing person's report? You said it yourself. Your dad is a dick."

Collin let out a puff of air and ran his fingers through his brown hair. "I won't argue that, but he's still our *dad*. He still *loves* us. Truth is, he thinks he's teaching Darla a lesson. He thinks that if she's out in the real world for a week or two, she'll realize how immature she's being and come back home. That's a lot easier to believe than that he killed her, isn't it?"

I guess when he put it that way, it did make sense, especially if his dad truly thought she was still alive. But I still couldn't shake my suspicions of him. I whispered, but my words came out sounding more like a hiss. "Why is it so easy to believe she's dead but so hard to believe that your dad killed her?"

Collin pursed his lips. "I already had my suspicions. She didn't take anything with her. I've checked her room, and I know my sister well enough to know what she would and wouldn't leave behind." Collin leaned in across the table, lowering his voice. "Maybe it's stupid, but my sister was into snow globes. She had a huge collection. There was this one that was really special to her that she got from my mom when she was little. When she was gone for four days last year, she had taken it with her. It's the one thing she wouldn't leave behind if she was going somewhere, but she left it behind. My dad doesn't seem to notice. He says it's just a stupid snow globe." Collin let out another sigh. "But to say my dad killed her, that's just stepping over a line. I'm not just saying that because he's my dad. I know he's not a killer."

The serious look in Collin's eyes told me that I was completely wrong to suspect his father.

"Trust me," he insisted.

And I did, to some extent. Granted, I didn't exactly trust his father, but I trusted Collin's judgement. In that moment, I was just about as certain as he was that his father didn't do it.

"I'm sorry I suggested it," I told him honestly.

"It's fine, as long as you believe me. It wasn't my dad, but if any of this is true—anything you heard in the bathroom—we have to do something for my sister. We have to find her."

"I agree," Savannah whispered from next to me, "but how do you suggest we do that?"

"Well, rumors tend to have an origin. What if this one is true? We'll start at the bluff."

"What?" I nearly choked. "Collin…" I couldn't tell him that I'd already thought of that and had been there multiple times already to scope it out and hadn't found anything, except I couldn't help but wonder if we'd find something with three people covering more ground.

"You guys are busy tonight, right? Kai, you have work? Savannah, you have play practice? We'll meet up tomorrow morning, okay? That way we'll have enough daylight to search the place."

I could hardly believe this was happening, yet I couldn't find the courage to tell them that his plan would probably lead us nowhere. Still, there was the tiniest bit of hope that it might take us somewhere.

"Okay," I heard myself say.

14

Instead of going on my run after work, I packed up my overnight bag and walked to Savannah's house. I could see her twirling a strand of blue hair around her finger from her second story window as I approached the house. She was holding her cell phone up to her ear. Just as I stepped onto the lawn, her eyes caught mine, and she waved. She had already bolted to the front door before I made it up the walkway.

"Kai!" she greeted excitedly.

I took my shoes off at the door and dropped my bag in the entryway. "Hi. What are you up to?"

"Oh, nothing special. I was just talking to my *boyfriend*. Ready for the trampoline?"

I definitely was. I needed something to relieve the stress.

Savannah led the way to her back yard and flipped on the patio light. It wasn't dark yet, but who knew how long we'd be out here?

"I've been practicing. Watch this." Savannah climbed onto the trampoline in her socks and bounced a few times. "Okay. Are you ready?"

"Ready as I'll ever be."

"Okay, here I go." She bounced higher. Then, her body flew backward as she pulled her legs to her chest and completed one rotation, landing perfectly on her feet before bouncing a few more times to slow her momentum.

I clapped in response. "That's awesome!"

"You try," she insisted, but no way was I trying *that*. I'd probably land on my head and break my neck or something.

"Uh, I think I'll stick with front flips." I hopped up on the trampoline and showed her my best front flip. I managed to successfully land on my feet rather than my butt like I was prone to doing.

We spent the next two hours jumping and laughing. At least it made up for the run I was missing. At one point, Savannah's cat, Mr. Meow, came outside, and we put him on the trampoline with us and tried to get him to jump. He did *not* like that. You couldn't even make out his orange stripes as he tore around the side of the house.

Savannah and I plopped down on our backs, too wiped out to jump anymore.

"I think my legs have turned to Jell-O," she complained.

"Yeah, working out will do that to you," I teased.

"Hey, I work out."

"I guess if you count carrying around those two ton weights with you everywhere you go."

Savannah furrowed her brow in confusion, but when she realized what I meant, her face relaxed. "Oh, shut up." She swatted at me lightly. "My boobs aren't *that* big."

"If you say so."

She rolled on her side and rested her head in her hand. Her expression turned serious when she looked at me.

"What?" I asked.

"I've been thinking."

"Uh-oh."

She swatted at me again. "Hey, I'm trying to be serious here."

I sighed and shifted to face her before resting my own head in my hand. "I'm sorry. Okay. What have you been thinking about?"

"Just about the whole Darla thing. It's all so…surreal."

My whole body tensed. Immediately, worry overcame me. I hadn't made my story about the girls in the bathroom believable, had I? Except that telling Savannah I could *astral travel* didn't sound any more believable. I finally let my breath out when Savannah continued speaking.

"I have another theory."

I shifted on the trampoline, which sent our bodies bouncing slightly. "About what?"

She twisted the charm Shawn had given her around in her fingers but didn't meet my gaze. "About Darla."

What? How could Savannah have a theory that I didn't? She didn't even know anything. Then again, what did I really know?

"What are you thinking?" I asked slowly.

She swallowed, like telling me was too hard for her. "Please don't be mad at me."

"What? Why would I be mad at you?"

"Just tell me you won't be mad."

"Okay. I won't be mad."

She lowered her voice even though no one else was around. When she spoke, I swear to God the earth stopped. "What if it was Collin?"

I could have been holding my breath for a mere second, or it could have been eons. I had no way of knowing because in that moment, it felt like time itself was standing still. After a long, dramatic pause that I couldn't quite measure, I finally began breathing again and managed to speak. My voice felt hoarse and scratchy in my throat. "What would make you say that?"

"I don't know. It's just…he's so insistent that his dad didn't do it. What if that's because he knows who really did?"

DISTANT DREAMS

I must have felt the same way Collin had when I
told him I suspected his father. Pain and anger coursed
through my veins, almost like Savannah had accused *me*
of such evil. Collin was sweet. We'd connected. We
could talk in a way that I hadn't been able to with
anyone but Savannah. The guy wasn't capable of
murder.

"That's crazy," I told her.

She raised her brows. "Is it? Because that theory
you came up with about his dad, he could have easily
had the same motive. Plus, I didn't see him at the dance
or after party, so what if that means he doesn't have an
alibi?"

Oh, my God. No. Collin wouldn't be *that* mad at his
sister. He wouldn't have followed her to the bluff when
she decided to run away. But, then again, I'd thought his
dad had done the same thing.

"Savannah, he wants to find her. Would a murderer
want to find his sister?"

She shrugged. "Maybe that's not his real motive.
Maybe he's trying to make sure we don't find anything.
You know, keep your friends close but your enemies
closer."

My stomach suddenly felt empty. "You don't think
Collin is actually capable of something like that, do
you?"

"I don't know the guy. I don't know what he's
capable of. I know he's big enough to overpower Darla,
though."

"Come on, Savannah. Listen to yourself. That's crazy."

"Is it, though? Collin told you the same thing about his dad, yet that made some sense, didn't it? Do you even really know Collin? I mean, think about it. You run up to the bluff every day after work, and just this week you two start running into each other? Right after Darla goes missing? And the rumor says she was murdered on that very same bluff? Maybe he's there making sure no one is snooping around."

It felt like my insides were turning to mush. It couldn't be Collin, except the more Savannah talked, the more it became believable.

"What would be his motive?"

Savannah shrugged again. "Darla was leaving. She was breaking up their family. His mom did the same thing, didn't she? It was like a repeat of his mom's abandonment. I'm not saying that he intended to do it, but what if it made him angry? Enough anger can change a person, make them do things they'd regret."

"Stop," I insisted. Savannah was making too much sense. "Just stop." I pushed to a seated position and slid across the trampoline to the edge. "I'm going to need a minute to think." I nearly whispered the words before jumping down and heading inside. I locked myself in the bathroom, and that's when the flood of tears came.

Could it really be him? I asked myself. *Does Collin have it in him?*

We were only starting to become friends, but I'd

known him for years. We were on the same sports team, and I didn't just know him as the best runner on the team. He always had the best sportsmanship, too. Could a guy that nice on the trails really be so evil when it came to his personal life?

No, I told myself. People who run are happy people. Exercise releases endorphins. He wouldn't do it. My reasoning was silly, but this was *Collin* we were talking about. I leaned against the bathroom sink and closed my eyes, picturing his sweet smile and soft brown eyes behind my lids. I moved to sit on the toilet lid and buried my face in my hands.

Savannah knocked on the door once to ask if I was okay. All I could do was cry into my hands and tell her I'd be out shortly. My voice wavered and cracked, a clear indication of my current condition.

"Okay. You come out when you're ready," she told me.

After I had wiped away all the tears and blew my nose, I finally emerged from the bathroom. Savannah was sitting against the wall in the hall, poking at her phone. She looked up at me when the door swung open and quickly stashed her phone away in her hoodie pocket.

"You okay?" she asked.

I nodded. "Let's go up to your room."

We passed by her parents in the living room and said hello before heading upstairs.

Savannah's room looked as if a fairy had barfed on

it. Lavender walls served as the backdrop to a very pink and purple color scheme. A pale purple canopy hung above her bed and sparkled with glitter when you turned on the light. The mirror at her desk was practically as tall as she was, and an extensive makeup collection occupied the near entirety of the desk's surface. A plush pink area rug spread out over her floor, and a nearly identical pink mushroom chair sat in the corner.

I plopped into the pink chair when I entered the room.

"Are you okay?" Savannah asked again as she crossed the room and fell onto her bed.

"I am. I'm just…thinking."

"Care to share?"

"If what you're saying is true, that Collin…" I couldn't bear to finish that sentence. "What do we do tomorrow? He asked us to meet him at the bluff."

Savannah pressed her lips together in thought. "Well, we can't not go."

My eyebrows came together. "Why not?"

"Then he'll know we're on to him. As long as we play dumb, he won't suspect that we suspect anything."

"Way to make that sentence confusing, Savannah."

She rolled her eyes. "You know what I mean. He can't know we're on to him."

I sighed. "You're right. I guess we're going to have to go meet up with him at the bluff tomorrow morning."

* * *

The thought of meeting up with a murderer churned my insides, and I didn't feel like I could eat breakfast.

"Isn't it dangerous to go?" I asked Savannah in the morning, still only half believing her theory.

"It's dangerous *not* to go," she told me as she smeared a dark line of makeup across her eye. She turned to me from the mirror. "If we don't go, he'll realize that we know. That could put us in more danger."

"You really think it could be him?"

She twisted her mouth to the side without saying anything. After turning back to the mirror, she finally spoke. "I don't know what to believe. Are you sure those girls you heard in the bathroom were serious?"

I swallowed the lump in my throat. How much longer could I hang onto this lie? "I have no doubt that Darla Baxter was murdered on that bluff."

"How would the girls even know?" She drew in a breath and paused her makeup routine. "Do you think they had something to do with it?"

I couldn't meet her gaze. Instead, I bent to my overnight bag and began shuffling through it, looking for nothing in particular. "I don't know how they knew, but it didn't sound like they were a part of it. I think they just heard someone talking about it or something."

Savannah resumed drawing lines on her face. "Well, why hasn't it gotten around school yet?"

My tone came out snarkier than I intended. "Maybe because the girls are like me and don't blab about everything they hear to everyone they know."

I couldn't be sure, but I thought I saw Savannah wince as if I'd personally attacked her. The truth was, she was kind of a blabber mouth, but at least she could keep a secret if asked to.

"Plus," I added. "I only heard the girls talking on Thursday. That didn't give much time for anyone to spread it around." I shifted through my memory, wondering for a moment if that matched the original story I told them. If it didn't, Savannah didn't seem to notice.

"Please." She rolled her eyes. "It could make it around school in a heartbeat if it was put in the hands of the right people."

I turned to her. "Well, let's make sure that doesn't happen."

She set down her eyeliner but continued to stare into the mirror. "If it's true, what does it matter?"

I sighed. "Because then people will start making assumptions. People could get hurt."

Savannah shifted to stare at me. "People already got hurt. Darla. Isn't it worth exposing the killer so he doesn't strike again?"

I moved to sit on Savannah's bed. "You still think it was Collin?"

She pressed her lips together. "I think it makes as much sense as the other two theories you had."

Hearing that sent an ill sensation to the pit of my stomach. I took a breath to compose myself. "Well, like you said, we have to go meet up with him. I really don't think we'll find anything, though. It's been a week already."

Savannah froze for a moment. "How do you know how long it's been? Everyone thought she was sick on Monday, and no one heard about her running away until Tuesday, so how can we be sure when she left?"

I didn't breathe for a second as I concocted an excuse in my head. "I thought I told you everything," I feigned. "The girls said it happened Saturday night on the bluff, after the homecoming dance and after party." A moment after I came up with the lie, I realized I could have said Collin told me.

"You didn't say that," Savannah accused.

"You just weren't listening." As soon as I said it, I hated myself. Why was I turning this around on her when I was the one to blame? I was the one lying to my friends.

"Dang," she said, moving to her dresser to find her clothes for the day. "If that's true, that makes things harder."

"Why?" I shifted on her bed to face her as she walked around the room.

"Didn't it rain on Sunday? That means it will be harder to spot the scene of the crime."

Oh. That made a lot more sense now. That's why I didn't see any blood afterward. The rain had washed it away.

I swallowed. "Like I said, I don't think we'll find anything."

Savannah sat on her bed next to me. "Hey, I know we have to go meet up with Collin, but afterward…"

"What?" I prodded.

"Afterward, do you think we should go to the police?"

I didn't answer for a long time. It sounded like such a logical course of action, but I had no doubt Jack would just accuse me of lying again. After all, I was already lying about how I came across the information. Then they'd want to know who the two girls I'd made up were, and of course, I couldn't tell them that.

"Honestly? I don't think they'd believe us," I told her. "With her leaving a note and her dad not wanting to file a missing person's report, they'll just say she's an adult who is free to leave if she wants."

Savannah dropped her shoulders. "Oh. Well, should we go?"

"Savannah." I grabbed her by the arm before she could make it too far from the bed. "Be nice to Collin, okay? I don't think he did it." Even as I said the words to reassure myself, I couldn't help but think that he was just as likely to have killed his sister as anyone.

15

Collin greeted us when we made it to the parking lot at the top of the bluff. "Thank you both for coming."

The knot in my chest eased when I saw him. I exchanged a glance with Savannah as if to say, *See? Look how sweet he is.*

"So," she asked, "what is it that we're looking for?"

"Anything," Collin answered. "I figured we could all split up. Keep an eye out for anything out of the ordinary: upturned leaves, blood, broken twigs, a body. Anything."

A shiver traveled down my spine when he spoke the words "a body."

"I was thinking I could sort of zig-zag my way down this part of the bluff." He pointed behind him. "Someone could take the other side of the road, and then someone could take up here and over by the cliff." Collin pulled out his phone. "Let's trade numbers so we can call if we find anything."

I took my phone out of my pocket. When I glanced over at Savannah, I noticed her hands were shaking. I lightly elbowed her in the ribs to tell her to take it easy.

"We'll meet back here in maybe an hour if no one finds anything. Sound good?" Collin asked once we had each other's numbers programmed in our phones.

"Yep," I answered while Savannah remained silent, staring at Collin with wide eyes.

He turned from us and made his way to his section of the bluff. I was just about to start toward the other side of the steep slope when Savannah grabbed my arm.

"Are you crazy?" she hissed. "We're not splitting up! He could come after one of us. Maybe that was his plan all along."

I jerked my arm from her grasp. "You don't still believe it was him, do you?"

She didn't answer, but the look in her eyes told me she wasn't sure.

"Fine," I told her. "We'll stick together."

Collin had already disappeared into the trees.

"Where do you suggest we start?" Savannah asked.

I didn't even have to think about it. "There." I pointed to the bush of death.

I knew it was silly to return there. I had already been there three times investigating and hadn't found a smidgen of evidence. Then again, I didn't think we'd actually find anything at *all*. Starting at the bush of death was my best option right now. It didn't surprise me that nothing showed up when Savannah and I began scouting the area. We spent a good ten minutes combing the grass around the parking lot before venturing into the trees that separated the parking lot from the clearing. Eventually, we made our way to the clearing but with no luck finding any clues.

"What is it we're supposed to be looking for again?" Savannah asked.

"Clues," I answered simply. "Want to try the side of the bluff by that path?" I pointed. It was the path I always came up when running. "We can't stay on the trail if we hope to find something."

"Okay," she agreed.

We treaded lightly through the leaves. While my footsteps were fairly quiet, Savannah's sounded like some massive wild animal's.

I braced myself against a tree to keep from sliding down the slope. "Savannah," I hissed, "you're kicking up leaves everywhere you go. Be careful. We don't want to mistake your footsteps for a clue."

"Oh, sorry." She began stepping with the balls of her feet, which helped. After a while, she spoke up again. "I have no idea what I'm supposed to be looking for. I'm not a tracker!"

"I know." I tiptoed forward. "Just keep an eye out for anything that may seem unusual."

"Did you hear Collin before?" she asked, stepping

lightly around a tree. "He was like, 'We're looking for a body.' You don't think she could still be out here, do you?"

I held my breath, still pushing forward. "Well, you think he's the one who did it. Would he really suggest that to us if he did it?"

She narrowed her eyes in thought. "No, I guess not."

We both went silent again for a long time before heading back up the bluff and checking out a few more areas of trees we hadn't looked through. When we were a few minutes away from the hour mark, we returned to the parking lot. Two cars were now parked there, and we watched a group of four guys from our school pile out of one of them before they headed down on the path toward the clearing.

Savannah took a seat in the grass next to the bush of death, and as much as I didn't want to sit *right there*, I found a spot beside her.

She lowered herself onto her back like she was exhausted. "Are you sure you heard the girls say it happened on the bluff?"

I paused for a second in confusion but then nodded when I realized she was referring to the lie I'd told her. "I'm sure."

"Well, it doesn't appear there's anything to find. Maybe we should head home before he comes back." Savannah swiveled her head to the side and pressed her cheek to the grass to take in her surroundings.

"He's not dangerous," I practically whispered.

She turned her head my way and then pulled her chin upward to look behind her. "Well, maybe—" Savannah's words instantly came to a halt, and she rolled over on her belly. Her eyes locked on something near the patch of trees.

I followed her gaze but didn't see anything.

"Oh, my God. What is *that*?" She shuffled to her feet and hurried over to whatever it was she saw.

"What's what?" I followed behind her.

"That," she answered, crouching down next to the edge of the tree line. She pulled the underbrush and a few leaves away from a spot on the ground and grabbed onto something I couldn't see thanks to her body blocking my view.

"What? What is it?" My mind raced through the possibilities. Could it be the rock I'd been looking for before? Maybe it was one of Darla's shoes.

Savannah turned toward me with wide eyes. When I looked into her palm, my heart nearly stopped. Could it be Darla's?

"You don't think…" I started, but I trailed off before I could finish the sentence.

"That it's Darla's? It could be."

The phone in Savannah's hand certainly *looked* like something Darla would carry around. It was the latest smartphone with a slim pink case. Darla must have lost it in the struggle. I mentally kicked myself for not finding it earlier. Then again, the passing days of falling leaves would have only buried it more.

"Well, turn it on!" I nearly shouted.

"I'm trying," she insisted while holding down the power button.

"You think the rain fried it?"

She shrugged. "I'm pretty sure this model is water resistant, isn't it? No, I think it just ran out of power. And look, too. The screen is broken."

"Did you two find anything?" Collins voice called from behind us.

I whirled around the same time Savannah shoved the phone behind her back.

"No," she lied.

"What do you have there, then?" He finally closed in on us and stopped.

"Oh, this?" Savannah held the phone up. "It's my —"

"Oh, my God!" Collin snatched the device from Savannah's hands. "Where did you find this? This is my sister's phone!"

"Are you sure?" I asked, inching toward him.

He didn't take his eyes off the phone. "I'm sure. This is the phone case I bought her for her birthday."

Collin's eyes looked empty as he absorbed our find as reality. He had to sit down to take it all in. It was like, to him, this was confirmation of her death, like he didn't quite believe it until now. Collin's shoulders shook slightly while he stared at the phone in his hands. And then he couldn't hold it back any longer. A tear fell from his eye and landed on the screen before he folded his face into his legs and cried.

A lump rose to my throat. I shot Savannah a glare that said, *See, he isn't the killer!*

Her expression softened like she agreed with me.

I didn't say anything when I sat in the grass next to Collin and rested a hand on his shoulder. I couldn't tell if he was okay with it or if it bothered him because he didn't react. He simply continued to sob into his knees.

Savannah found her way to the opposite side of him and wrapped an arm around him. I knew it was more than just a comforting hug. It was an apology, an apology for accusing him of murder, even though he didn't know she'd done that.

After a long silence where no one spoke, Collin finally pulled in a deep breath and rubbed his tears away. "I'm sorry."

"You have nothing to apologize for," I assured him.

He let out a puff of air. "Guys aren't supposed to cry like this."

"That's sexist," Savannah told him, rubbing his shoulder. "You have every right to cry."

He sucked in another long breath. "I know I kind of hated her on one level, but she was also kind of like a mom to me. She was only a year and a half older, but still."

Savannah and I leaned in closer to him, both rubbing his back. In any other situation, this might seem awkward, but in that moment, it felt completely natural to comfort him.

"It's just that—" Collin started, but a scream cut through the air, stopping his words in their tracks.

I immediately jumped to my feet and ran along the path that led to the clearing. *Not again!* I thought.

Collin followed behind me. "Kai," he called.

When I broke through the trees, I instantly noticed three of the four guys I had seen earlier. They were all on the opposite side of the wooden barrier just inches from the edge of the cliff, looking over.

Oh, my God. They pushed the other guy into the river!

"Hey!" I called, quickly making my way over to them. I didn't know what I expected to happen next or where my sudden bout of courage came from.

All three guys caught my eye, but one of them didn't slow down. He removed his shirt and turned back toward the water. Before I could process what was going on, he flung himself off the edge of the cliff.

My gut wrenched as if someone had punched me in the stomach. "NO!"

The other two guys looked at me and laughed.

I stopped when I made it to the barrier, not daring to go any further. I craned my neck to try to get a better view of the guy who had just fallen, but I couldn't see him. Collin finally caught up to me and grabbed my arm. I whirled toward him, but my fright didn't waver.

"Calm down," he insisted.

I couldn't! My breath was on fire, and my pulse was racing.

"They're fine," he told me calmly. "They're just cliff jumping."

I drew in a breath and glanced back toward the two remaining boys. One laughed and met my eyes as he backed away from the edge. In the next moment, he was sprinting for it before the ground ended and his bare feet were thrashing in the air. All of the air left my lungs.

"Cliff jumping?" I asked breathlessly, turning to Collin. I'd seen plenty of people cross the barrier, but never before had I witnessed them jump off the cliff.

"Yes," he told me. "It's an adventure sport."

The fourth guy made his escape before I could truly process what Collin was saying. Once they were all gone, I finally noticed the pile of clothes they'd left behind, everything but their shorts. Oh. They weren't in any real danger. They were just having fun.

I sank to the ground like I was going to be sick. I hadn't even noticed Savannah was next to me until I saw her shadow.

"They could get hurt!" I cried.

"I know," Collin said. "That's the thrill of it, like skydiving. Remember how you told me you wanted to skydive?"

I only vaguely remembered telling him that. "Yeah, but you're in a harness with a parachute when you skydive. This is just…" I gestured to the cliff, unable to finish my sentence.

"They'll be fine. These guys do this all the time," he assured me.

"In the fall? Isn't the water cold?"

"It's actually really nice out today," Savannah pointed out.

Collin pulled me up from the ground, giving me another chance to assess the scene. I couldn't believe these guys *jumped off cliffs* for fun. As I stood, I noticed the sun was quite warm on my skin, and that's when I saw how high it had risen since we got here.

I gasped. "What time is it?" I pulled out my phone and looked at the time before anyone could answer. "I have to get to work."

At the very least, my breakdown over the cliff jumping guys had taken Collin's mind off his sister enough that he seemed more like himself. He slowly turned back toward the parking lot, and I followed behind him with Savannah at my side.

"Do you want to meet up later?" he asked as we walked.

"I have to work until six," I told him before glancing at Savannah. "Savannah has a date after that."

"Oh, that's fine then." He sounded disappointed.

"You two can hang out without me," Savannah said, which completely took me by surprise.

I shot her a quizzical glare as if to ask, *So, you think he's safe?*

She sent me back an expression that said, *He's obviously not the killer.*

Just like I'd been trying to tell her all along! He didn't know anything, and the way he broke down when he saw Darla's phone was a clear indication of that.

"I'll call you after work, Collin," I told him. "We can meet up then."

A hint of a smile crossed his face. "Thanks. I look forward to it."

I didn't say anything, but I truly looked forward to it, too.

16

The doorbell rang just as I finished shoving the rest of Braden's crap into the cabinet under the TV. Gaming controllers and DVDs had scattered the floor just moments ago. Collin didn't need to see how untidy my house normally was.

I rushed to the door and took a deep, calming breath before opening it. Seeing Collin standing on my porch seemed so surreal, like he didn't quite fit into my personal life.

"Collin." I smiled.

"Hi, Kai," he said as he stepped into my living room. "I brought you something." He held a bag of chips and a jar of nacho cheese out to me.

I took them from him warily. "What's this for?"

He shrugged. "It's my comfort food. I thought you

might like it, too."

I eyed the can of nacho cheese. Salsa con Queso, it said. Medium. Just the way I liked it. "It sounds delicious. I think we have some meat in the freezer and taco seasoning. We could make it deluxe."

"Mm." Collin rubbed his belly for show, making me laugh.

"Come on." I crossed the living room and set the food on the kitchen counter.

"Kai," my mom called as she walked down the hall. "Who was at the door?"

Her words trailed off when she saw Collin standing in the kitchen. He *so* didn't fit in here. His long, toned legs left him towering at six foot, and the brown hair that fell into his equally dark eyes was much in contrast to my family's pale complexion. Mom and Braden had blonde hair and blue eyes while I had red hair and green eyes, and none of us were exactly tall at five-foot-six.

It wasn't just that, either. His jeans almost looked as if they'd been pressed, and they were in perfect condition without a single hole or fray. Whereas my family's casual attire was a typical t-shirt, Collin wore an untucked button-down shirt with casual rolled up sleeves. I found his style somewhat attractive, and apparently so did my mom when her eyes nearly bulged out of her skull.

"So *this* is the friend you told me was coming over." She raised her brows like she was impressed. Then she turned to Collin. "Hi, I'm Lisa."

He extended his hand. My mother held out hers as if expecting him to shake it, but instead, he brought her hand to his lips and kissed it. I nearly fell over in embarrassment, and it didn't help when my mother's cheeks flamed red and she giggled like a little school girl.

Braden emerged from his bedroom just then to see what all the commotion was about.

Oh, God, Braden, I thought. *Don't do it*.

"Hey," Braden said. "Are you Kai's *boyfriend*?"

I shoved my face into my hands in embarrassment before taking a deep breath and letting them fall back at my side. "No, Braden. He's just a friend. And we're making dinner together, so if you don't *mind*, we could use some space in the kitchen."

"What are you making?" Braden inquired. He immediately stepped around the counter so we had even *less* space in the kitchen.

"Nachos," Collin answered before I could tell Braden to bug off. "Want to help?"

I instantly shot Collin a glance to let him know I didn't want Braden's help, but he didn't catch it.

"Nah, it's okay. I cook all the time. I think it's Kai's turn."

I pursed my lips and glared at Braden, but he ignored me.

"Braden," my mom said, gripping his shoulders and leading him out of the kitchen. "Let's give them some space. Thanks for making dinner, Kai," she shouted back.

"No problem." I breathed, relieved that my family had left us with some semblance of privacy. "Let's see what we have." I opened the freezer and set some of its contents on the counter before finally spotting a package of ground beef.

"So, your family," Collin started while I returned the contents of the freezer back to their proper spot. "They're nice."

I nearly choked on my laugh. "They're... something."

"Yeah," Collin said, running his fingers through the ends of his hair. "I get what you mean. They're family. No one likes their own family."

"That's not true!" I defended. "I like them. I just..." How could I finish that sentence?

"I get it. I just wish I would have shown my sister more love when I had the chance." Collin's face fell when he spoke about his sister, and so did my heart in response.

If I lost Braden or my mom, I'd be devastated even though we bickered all the time. Suddenly, Collin's statement made me want to rush down the hall and pull my family into a big hug, but I refrained from doing so for fear of appearing crazy.

"I'm sorry," was all I could say as I began shuffling through the cupboards in search of other nacho toppings. Collin took the initiative to thaw the meat in the microwave, and I found an old can of black olives

I'd forgotten we had.

He shifted nervously next to the counter. "Can I ask you something?"

I glanced up at him before digging through the drawer next to me for the can opener. "Sure."

He raked his fingers through his hair again but didn't say anything for a long time. I thought maybe he'd changed his mind and wasn't going to ask the question anymore, but I noticed how he continued to shift uncomfortably out of the corner of my eye. It was like he was trying to work up the courage to spit out the words.

I paused to set the can opener down next to the olives and turned to Collin. "Are you okay?"

Just then, the timer on the microwave beeped, and Collin checked the meat before putting it back in for another minute. "That depends on your definition of 'okay.'" He rocked his weight between his feet. "Here's the thing…Can you be honest with me?"

I nodded. "Yes."

He went silent for a beat before finding the courage to speak up. "Does Savannah think I had something to do with Darla's disappearance?"

My body tensed, and I immediately turned back to my can of olives, twisting almost too violently on the can opener. "What would make you say that?" My voice quivered.

Before I knew what was happening, Collin's hand wrapped around my wrist gently, stopping me. His fingers were warm, almost comforting. My gaze met his before falling back down to our hands. I paused and wondered what I was going to say to him.

He spoke first. "It's just the way she was acting today. She seemed…I don't know…wary of me, and then she didn't want to show me Darla's phone." Collin released his grip on my wrist and leaned back against the counter. "Then she was being nice to me, so I don't really get it. I wasn't sure…" His voice trailed off.

I finally looked up at him again. "It's nothing, really. She just had this stupid theory that clearly isn't true."

He seemed to stand up straighter. "What kind of theory?"

The tension in my muscles grew. What could I possibly say without hurting his feelings? "It was just a suggestion, really. She was just thinking of all options, and you were close to Darla, so…"

Collin nodded like he understood, but the expression on his face communicated pain.

"She doesn't think that anymore," I assured him, although I wasn't sure the statement made him feel any better. It only implied that she used to think he was guilty. "We saw how you reacted when you saw the phone, and it was obvious. You miss your sister. You're not capable of something like—"

"You suspected me, too?" Collin interrupted as soon as he absorbed what I was saying.

Honestly, I had never truly thought he was guilty,

but I can't say the possibility that he might be a suspect never crossed my mind. "Not like that, Collin. Savannah made some sense, and she pointed out that you didn't have an alibi for that night, but I defended you." I stepped toward him, although I didn't know what I'd do once I closed the short distance between us.

Collin quickly straightened up, and I recoiled. "It's fine." Though he claimed he was fine, his expression confirmed that I'd hurt him on some level. "As long as you know now that that's not the case. I don't think you'd invite me into your house if you thought it was." After a pause, he spoke again. "And for the record, I was staying at Ian's that night because neither of us wanted to go to the dance. He'll tell you I was at his house all night. I didn't know anything happened until I came home and found the note."

At this point, I suspected Collin was babbling to try to convince me of his innocence, but I was already convinced before he'd started speaking.

"Collin," I said firmly, locking my eyes on his and willing him to look at me. When he did, I continued. "I believe you are a good person. I do not think you could have done that to your sister." I couldn't bring myself to use the words 'killed' or 'murdered.' "I know you didn't do it. The problem is that we still have to find something that will convince your dad and the police that there's reason to worry about her."

His expression softened, making him look more like himself. The tension in my shoulders eased.

"Yeah, no. You're right." He pressed the button on the microwave to open the door and check on the frozen meat again. I hadn't even noticed the timer had gone off. "By the way, I tried charging Darla's phone to see what I could find on it."

"And?" I asked hopefully. Perhaps there was something we could give to the police.

"Well, it charged, but the screen wouldn't work. It's cracked, and the backlight won't turn on. I'm going to get it fixed, but the guy I took it to said they have to order parts. I won't have it back for a couple of days."

My heart sank in my chest. That meant the next few days would be a waiting game and that we were no closer to finding evidence of Darla's murder.

"Collin, I'm sorry." My voice came out as a whisper. I wasn't sure if he heard me or simply chose to ignore me because the next thing I knew, we were frying up meat and cutting up olives without saying another word about Darla. Aside from the meat and olives, I managed to dig up a can of refried beans, but we were short lettuce, salsa, and sour cream. Collin didn't seem to mind.

"Dinner," I called to my family.

Braden put in a movie while we ate. I wasn't surprised that my mom didn't stick around for the whole thing. Once the credits started rolling, Braden escaped back into his bedroom, leaving Collin and me alone in the living room.

I shifted nervously on the couch, unsure of what to

say to him. I glanced at the clock and then out the window.

"Hey, Collin. Shouldn't you be getting home?"

"Huh?"

My fingers knotted around the ends of my sleeves in my lap. "I just—I heard your dad say he didn't want you out after dark or something. Is that your curfew?"

"Oh, no," he told me. "It's not like that. I can stay out. He just doesn't want me running in the dark. He's scared I'm going to get hurt. I don't know if you know my stats this year, but I've slowed down a bit."

What? I didn't know that. He was always the fastest one on the team. "What do you mean?"

"It was a couple of months ago. I had just started running outside again when the weather got warmer. I was running at night up around the bluff. There's not a lot of light up there, and I didn't bring a flashlight or head lamp or anything. I didn't realize I'd be out so late." He took a breath before continuing. "So I couldn't see, and I stupidly tripped over a root on the path. I did a lot of damage to the muscles and tendons in my ankle. It cost my dad a ton in physical therapy so I could run again for the cross country season. I can run again, but I'm just not as good as I was before. My dad doesn't want me running at night because he's afraid I'll hurt myself."

"Collin, I had no idea." I inched closer to him on the couch without consciously deciding to. How was it that I'd drifted so far away from my old cross country teammates that I didn't even know when one of them got hurt?

"It was my fault," he said disappointedly, "but I've fallen behind a lot of the other runners. I'm not the fastest on the team anymore. That's one of the reasons I run after practice. I feel like I need the extra practice if I'm going to ever be as good as I used to be."

Now it made sense why he seemed slower than I remembered when we ran together.

"It will get better, you know," I told him, even though I wasn't entirely sure.

"I'm sure it will," he agreed. "I just hate myself for being so stupid."

"Hey, don't say that. It could have happened to anyone."

Collin raised his brows. "Do you ever run in the dark without a light?"

I shrugged. "I have a couple of times. I run at twilight."

He went silent for a beat. "Maybe we should run together more. You might be faster than me now." He winked, sending my heart fluttering.

I let out a light laugh. "I doubt that, but I'm up for a challenge sometime."

He extended his hand. "Deal."

I shook it with a smile. The room went silent again, leaving me too much time for thoughts to swim around in my mind.

"So." Collin elongated the word to ease the

awkwardness, not that it helped. "What do you want to do now?"

I shifted to sit on my feet. "I want to ask you something."

"Okay."

"I don't mean to bring the topic up again, but I just can't stop thinking about your sister, and I want to help you find closure."

Collin nodded, encouraging me to continue.

"Is there anything you can tell me about who Darla's boyfriend might be? I mean, do you know anything or have suspicions?"

"What do you mean?"

"If he was secret, maybe she met him online or something. Did she ever talk about a guy or maybe act secretive around a computer or something?"

Collin shook his head. "I'm hoping her phone will tell us something about him. If they were an item, she would have texted him. I checked her Facebook and other profiles but couldn't find any friend or anything who could be her boyfriend. I can't say I ever had any suspicions that she was dating anyone. As far as I knew, she'd basically cut everyone off last year with her friends' falling out."

Suddenly, something clicked in my head. If Darla had a falling out with her friends, that meant that she had enemies. What if one of them was the killer? "What was all that about again?" I asked.

He let out a long sigh. "I don't really know. She was

my sister, but it's not like we talked much about it. Here's what I know. Last year at homecoming, she was wearing the same dress as the homecoming queen. You know how the kids at our school have this tradition of blindfolding and locking the king and queen up in a closet at the after party?"

I nodded, instantly reminded of all the gossip that was going around after the homecoming dance this year, how Anna Evans didn't want to go in the closet with Hunter Murphy.

"Well," Collin continued, "apparently my sister was mistaken for the homecoming queen last year, and they blindfolded her. No one noticed because they were wearing the same dress. I can see the mistake because they both had dark hair, too. But still…"

So that's why the whole thing with Anna and Hunter sounded familiar to me. I had heard bits of this story before, but I hadn't realized Darla was in the middle of the drama last year.

"So, why did her friends all ditch her then?" I asked.

He shrugged. "I don't know the story well enough. First, Shawn got really mad because she made out with another guy, and then I guess all her friends just followed him. They thought she was a cheater, but that wasn't really it."

"What do you mean?"

"My sister basically went into a depression after that. I saw a lot of it, you know, because we live

163

together. She was really broken up about Shawn leaving her, and I don't think she would have risked their relationship. She really loved him."

"What are you suggesting?"

He pressed his lips together in thought. "I'm not really suggesting anything. I think it was an honest mistake putting her in the closet with the homecoming king, and I think her friends just wouldn't listen to her when she tried to explain that."

"Well, did she even do anything with him?"

He shrugged. "Don't know. I wasn't there."

We both went quiet for a moment before I spoke again. "Do you think one of her old friends still had something against her? Maybe we should consider them as suspects."

Collin sighed. "I have no idea. Like I said, she didn't exactly talk to me about it all. I think we should wait to get her phone back and see if we can find anything on there. It may still be her boyfriend."

Great. A waiting game was just what I needed to ease my anxiety. Not. But what other choice did I have?

17

Just as I predicted, the waiting game that followed the next week did *not* ease my anxiety. If anything, it only left me more troubled as the recurring nightmare continued to haunt me.

On Sunday morning before work, I tried the route Collin already took in stalking Darla's Facebook and Twitter profiles. I failed to come up with any answers as to who might be her mystery boyfriend. If she wanted him to be a secret, she did a pretty good job of it. I wondered if maybe they'd connected on a dating site or something, which would mean there weren't public comments about their relationship.

As I scrolled through Darla's feed, sadness knotted in my chest. No one had posted on her profiles in the last few days. I had to wonder what people would do if they knew she was dead. Surely they'd leave tons of posts on her timeline telling her how much they missed her and how sad it was she was gone, even though most of those people didn't care about her when she was alive. I mean, sure, people cared that she had popularity status, and that's why they voted her on homecoming court this year, but if what Collin had told me was true, she didn't have many *real* friends to rely on in the past year.

After a long Sunday alone with my thoughts, I was thankful to have Savannah keep me company in the morning before school on Monday. We sat across from each other at a table in the commons.

"Your hair is still blue," I pointed out to her. "I thought for sure it'd be purple or green this week."

"Ew. I'm never dying my hair green." She tugged at the ends of her hair to inspect the color. "I have to dye it brown for my costume, so I figured there's no reason to do another color before then. My mom's going to strip the color and dye it brown Wednesday night. Besides, Shawn likes it blue."

My brows shot up. "Really? I would have thought he'd be the kind of guy who preferred…" My voice trailed off. Honestly, I didn't know what Shawn would prefer. I didn't really know anything about the guy. "So, how'd your date go?"

Savannah nearly melted into her chair. "It was perfect. He took me out of town to eat at this fancy sit-down restaurant. Believe me, the place was better than anything we have in town."

"That's because we only have one fast food place here," I pointed out.

"Well, this was really good, and you'd be proud of me. I ate in front of him without getting embarrassed."

I had to refrain from rolling my eyes. I couldn't understand girls who were embarrassed to eat in front of other people. "What else did you do?"

She shrugged casually. "Oh, the usual first date. We went to the movies and made out a bit. He was a real gentleman. He didn't pressure me into anything."

"I would hope not! I'm glad you're happy with him, though."

She beamed. "I really am."

The bell rang just then, and we headed off to our lockers side-by-side. It was when I reached my first hour class that I heard the first whispers of Darla's death. I wasn't even paying attention to the conversations nearby, but when I heard the word "murdered," I immediately honed my attention on the voice across the room. It was Sara again.

"No way," she said. "I heard she ran away."

On one hand, I was shocked that it took this long for people to hear this rumor, but on the other, I was surprised it made the rounds at all considering the rumor basically originated from me and I'd only talked to Savannah and Collin about it. Except, which one of them would have told people? Certainly not Collin.

I breathed a sigh of relief when it sounded like the

group didn't know much. They didn't even mention the bluff, and they sounded completely unbelieving that it had happened at all. I mean, I wanted people to know at some point and mourn Darla, but I also didn't want the rumor to blow up to the point where we started hearing fake accusations and didn't know how to sort fact from fiction.

Sara shot down the conversation again. "That's just a stupid rumor. Someone must have made it up. Last week she ran away, this week she's dead. No way."

I raced to my locker between first and second period and found Savannah shuffling through her locker.

"Savannah," I hissed.

She jumped slightly.

"You didn't tell anyone about Darla, did you?"

Her eyes shifted between mine. "No, why?"

I relaxed. Some of the other students who were eating at Amberg Hamburg that day must have overheard despite our effort to talk in private. "I heard people talking about it, but they don't seem to believe it. Hopefully that means the rumor won't blow up."

Savannah's eyes narrowed. "And that's a good thing, why?"

"If we want to find some real evidence to show the police, I don't want people having preconceived ideas about what really went down." I picked at the edge of my tattered textbook, suddenly realizing the real reason I didn't want the rumor to spread just yet. "Honestly,

I—I don't want the police laughing us off." My gaze fell to my shoes. "If they hear it's just a rumor, they may not take us seriously." *Like they would take us seriously anyway*, my inner voice mocked. *At least this way we have a better chance*, another voice countered. "If you hear anything, can you please not indulge in the gossip?"

She nodded with a look in her eyes that told me she was doing this only because I asked. "My lips are sealed."

The rest of the school day came and went in a haze until I met up with Collin in the library during eighth period. Now that the waiting game had begun, neither of us mentioned Darla. It was like we both figured we'd exhausted the topic and wouldn't have anything more to say about it until her phone came back from the guy who was fixing the screen. Even so, it was nice to talk casually with Collin.

"Before he knew what happened, I sprinted past him in the last few seconds and hit the finished line before him." Collin recounted a cross country story from this season for me. It made me miss the sport deeply.

I smiled. "I bet he didn't like that."

"Are you kidding? Of course he didn't."

"Are you going to psych me out like that when we race?" I teased.

"Right. We still have that deal." He paused for a second in thought. "Nah, I'll play it fair."

"Shh," the librarian hissed at us across the room.

We lowered our voices and continued talking in whispers until the final bell rang.

Collin caught my attention before I could escape the library. "Do you maybe want to run with us at practice today? We only have one meet left, and Coach is getting kind of laid back now that it's the end of the season. I'm sure he wouldn't mind you tagging along. He'd probably love to see you back running with us."

I sighed. I really did miss the team and Coach Myers. "Sorry, but I have plans," I told him while we walked side-by-side to our lockers.

Collin's face fell, but he quickly recovered.

"I'm helping out with the play, and then I have to go to work."

He nodded. "Right. I knew that. Hey, maybe I'll check the play out on opening night."

"I'm not in it, you know."

He shrugged. "I know, but you're still a part of it."

I tucked a strand of red hair behind my ear when we reached my locker. "Okay, well, I hope to see you there."

A smile crept across Collin's face. "Okay. I'll see you. Bye, Kai."

"Bye." I waved as he made his way across the hall to his own locker.

"Ooh," Savannah's voice rang from beside me.

I quickly entered in my combination and hid my face in the locker while pretending to organize my textbooks. "Ooh, what?" I tried to sound nonchalant, but it didn't really work.

"You two seem to be getting close."

I almost smiled but quickly realized it and forced the grin off my face. "We're just friends." I finally looked at her after slinging my backpack over my shoulder and shutting my locker.

"Right." She elongated the word like she didn't believe me. "I have another study day in the library on Friday, so I'll have to watch you two kids and make sure you aren't getting too wild together."

"Hey, don't you have lines to run or something?" I teased only to change the subject.

"Yeah, all of my two lines? God, if I could just be Cinderella. I'd be pretty great in that role."

"I don't doubt that," I told her.

We reached the auditorium and went our separate ways. Since the set was done and Lindsay didn't seem to need my help, I sat by Tyler during rehearsal while he taught me the basics of how he managed the lights and sound. It was pretty dull, to say the least, but it killed time before I had to go to work, which again did nothing to help my unease.

When I returned home, I swear I could smell Jack in my house before I even entered the door. Sure enough, he was sitting at my kitchen table laughing with my mom. I gritted my teeth, not wanting to witness this scene again. Why was it that my mom never laughed with me?

I escaped to my bedroom and plopped down on my

bed. Although it felt like I hadn't done anything today, I was exhausted. I didn't intend to fall asleep, but I woke an hour and half later with drool pooling beneath me on the pillow. I wiped it away and glanced at the clock. Immediately, my heart lurched. I'd missed my chance at taking my after-work run, which meant I also missed crossing paths with Collin and meeting him on the bluff.

Okay, it's not like we were scheduled to meet on the bluff or like he expected me to be there or anything, but I still found myself disheartened that I'd missed him.

I sulked around the rest of the night, sadly flipping through my dream books and feeling sorry for myself that I couldn't astral travel anymore.

The next few days passed in much the same way. When I made my run on Tuesday, Collin wasn't there, which sent my heart sinking.

Wednesday was a dress rehearsal for the play, but I still had to work, so I left practice early like normal. I'd managed to get off for the dress rehearsal on Thursday and for opening night on Friday. Who knew moving sets could take so much out of you? I spent Thursday evening rushing from one side of the stage to the other. Lindsay had me help with costume changes when I wasn't moving pieces of the set.

"Kai, what are you so busy with?" Savannah kept asking me when she wasn't on stage, which was for most of the play. She sat on a chair in a corner of the dressing room most of the time, fiddling with her phone and twirling a strand of her now brown hair around her finger.

"I have to watch for my cues," I told her. "And Lindsay assigned me to some of the actors to make sure they're in the right place at the right time and that their costumes are where they're supposed to be."

"Whew," Savannah said, wiping fake sweat off her forehead dramatically. "Sounds like you're pretty busy."

I had a few breaks between scene changes where I sat in the auditorium chairs and watched the play to get a better feel for my cues. Even though he insisted we were going to do the whole thing without stopping, Mr. Spears paused a couple of times, mostly to chew out students who were goofing off backstage and causing a distraction.

"You can't be talking backstage tomorrow night," he kept telling the cast. They eventually shut up the third time he yelled at them. Then he had the actors on stage redo one scene when Tiana broke character and cursed under her breath for missing a line.

"I knew that line," Savannah bragged next to me.

I nearly jumped out of my skin, having not realized she was there. "Holy crap, Savannah!" I hissed in a whisper. "Warn me next time, will you?"

She shrugged like she didn't care. "I got bored in the dressing room. I only have two scenes. This sucks." She folded her arms across her chest.

"You'll get the lead next year. I know you will." Although I couldn't possibly know that, I was pretty confident it would happen. Savannah was a great actress.

I nearly forgot I was supposed to help Tiana into her Cinderella ball gown until she started calling my name. Since it was dress rehearsal, we had to practice everything, which meant the receiving line, too.

"Quick," she insisted.

I rushed after her into the dressing room and quickly pulled the dress off its hanger and unzipped the zipper. Tiana had already stripped off her peasant clothing. She hurried into the dress, and I pulled it up over her shoulders, forgetting at first about the faulty zipper she'd pointed out to me.

"Come on. Mr. Spears says we can't do this if we're not quick enough."

I managed to get the zipper up, and Tiana rushed off to the receiving line. Luckily for her, we did it quick enough that Mr. Spears approved and she was able to wow everyone with her beautiful ball gown.

After dress rehearsal, I was finally able to breathe a sigh of relief. This lasted only about ten minutes. I hadn't even left the school before I received Collin's text.

I'm picking up the phone now. Want to meet up?

Immediately, my heart began pumping wildly against the sides of my rib cage, and my fingers shook so much that I nearly dropped my phone. This could be it. We could find something on Darla's phone that could lead to her boyfriend. We might learn who he really is and be able to put a face and a name to her killer.

Yes, I managed to type. Where would we meet, though? I didn't really want to go to his house since his dad still gave me the creeps. *My house?* I suggested.

See you soon, he texted back.

"I thought you left already," Savannah said as she approached me in the school hallway. "What's up? You look like...I don't know...like something is on your mind."

I didn't know what emotions were showing on my face, but I quickly let my expression fall back to normal.

"It's Collin," I told her, waving my phone in my hand. "He just texted me."

Her eyebrows shot up. "And?"

I couldn't hide the hint of a smile twitching at the sides of my lips. "He's coming to my house."

"What?" she squeaked. "Tonight?"

"Yeah," I told her as we began walking. "He's headed to get the phone back."

Savannah put a hop into her step. "Can I come along?"

"Sure." I smiled.

As Savannah and I exited the school, my body came alive with nerves as I prepared to get answers.

18

Today, I was almost hoping Jack would be at my house so that if we found something on Darla's phone, we could show him right away, but it was practically the first night in weeks that Jack wasn't there. It was somewhat of a relief, too. The guy didn't trust me, and I didn't like him, either.

The doorbell rang, sending a shock of nerves through my body. I hoped to God there'd be something on Darla's phone that would put this whole mystery to rest.

"Collin," I greeted with a smile. This time when I saw him on my porch, it didn't feel so out of the ordinary.

"Hi, Kai," he said as he made his way into the house.

"Did you find anything yet?" I asked hopefully.

Collin shook his head. "No. I didn't even turn it on. I got it back and came over right away."

Savannah sat up a little straighter on the couch. "Let's see what we can find."

Mom and Braden were off in their rooms doing their own thing, so we had enough privacy in the living room. Besides, Mom probably wouldn't let me have a boy in my room anyway, even if Savannah was here.

Collin took a deep breath as he settled into the middle cushion on the couch and held down the power button on his sister's phone. The screen lit up, and the phone sang a short melody. I noticed the device shake slightly in his hands.

"You okay?" I asked.

He nodded. "I just—I don't know what we'll find. I still don't want to believe the rumors are true." He rubbed a hand over his face before the home screen loaded.

My heart hammered, but I was sure Collin's was pounding harder.

"Where do I look first?" His voice wavered.

"Facebook?" Savannah suggested.

Collin swiped the screen only to be prompted for a password.

I sucked in a deep breath. "Do you know the password?"

He shook his head. "I might be able to guess it, though." His fingers grazed over the screen. The first try was no good. He tried again, but it was to no avail. He paused for several seconds and stared into the distance. Finally, his eyes lit up, and he typed in a series of numbers that unlocked the screen.

I let out the breath I was holding. "What was the password?"

He gave a sly smile. "It was the date she and Shawn started dating. I remembered because it was two days before my birthday."

"That's weird," I stated rhetorically. If she had a new boyfriend, wouldn't she be over Shawn? "She must have not bothered to change it recently."

Collin clicked the Facebook icon, which brought up a new window that told him the app couldn't connect. It felt like our hearts sank in sync. How were we going to get any information?

"Woops. Her data must be turned off," Collin said, sending my body relaxing.

Of course. It was just a setting on the phone. We weren't at a complete loss for information. He flipped on the data setting and opened the Facebook app again. I didn't even notice when I leaned in closer to him to get a better look.

Collin immediately navigated to Darla's Facebook messages and scrolled through them, but there weren't any emails from our mystery guy. The few messages at the top were from what Collin told me were Darla's family members—an aunt and grandma—but as he scrolled further, the dates on the messages reached months into the past from some of Darla's friends. Eventually, we found messages from a year ago, where they appeared more frequently but were also insignificant to our current investigation.

Savannah gave an audible sigh when she realized that searching Facebook would be useless. "What other services did she use often? Try Twitter."

Collin did, but again, there wasn't anything out of the ordinary. When we exhausted her social media accounts, which I was sure would hold some hint of her mystery man but didn't, and flipped through all her apps to see what other services she used, Savannah finally suggested the obvious.

"Check her texts."

"Right." Collin closed the last app we looked at and navigated to the message folder.

My fingers quivered against my thighs in anticipation. As soon as her messages opened, my heart nearly stopped. Right there at the top was the last conversation Darla had before her death, dated less than an hour before I'd witnessed her last breaths. But it wasn't the timing of the messages that left my throat dry. The owner of the number texting Darla was listed as "Traitor" in her phone.

We all went silent for several long seconds. I finally tore my gaze from the screen and looked to Collin. "What does that mean?"

"I have no idea."

Savannah finally managed to speak. "Well, click on

the conversation! See what it says."

Collin did as he was told. He scrolled to the top of the conversation to view where it all started. Either Darla hadn't texted this number before or she'd deleted previous conversations because this one was short. It started the night of her death.

Hey, we need to talk, Traitor's message said.

No, we don't, Darla had texted back. *I have nothing to say to you. I'm over it. Have been for a long time.*

I have something to say to you.

Really? Because you had your chance.

I know, and I'm sorry. Can we talk? In person?

What? Right now?

Yes, this can't wait.

Darla didn't text back before Traitor returned another text. *Please.*

You can't be serious, Darla's text said. *You betrayed me.*

I know I did, but you need to hear the whole story.

Darla's next text sent two minutes later. *It's late. Do we need to do this now?*

Yes. Can we meet somewhere?

Darla's following text was timestamped six minutes later, like she had been contemplating whether or not to meet up with this person. *Fine. Where?*

The bluff?

That's where the texts ended. As soon as we were all done reading through the conversation, we exchanged glances. I forced down the lump in my throat and noticed Savannah do the same. A muscle popped in

Collin's jaw, but he relaxed before he spoke.

"Do you know what this means?" Collin's eyes glazed over but remained locked on the screen.

"Yeah," Savannah's voice quivered. "It means that whoever owns this number is the murderer."

I didn't speak for a long time, only let this newfound information sink in. The first thing I noticed was that it didn't make sense that Darla's boyfriend was the killer. Certainly *this* wasn't her boyfriend. If she *had* run away with him, she wouldn't be calling him "Traitor" in her phone. That's not to mention that this conversation didn't do anything to hint that she was running away.

Collin headed back to the main message screen as these thoughts swam through my mind. He began scrolling through the messages, but all the names were recognizable. There was nothing to name her mystery boyfriend.

How does he fit into this picture? I wondered. No one had heard of him. He didn't appear on any of Darla's social channels. She hadn't even texted him. Another few moments passed before the reality of the situation struck.

A sharp intake of breath passed my lips, but I was in too much shock to truly notice that I'd made a noise. Collin and Savannah stared at me expectantly.

I finally managed to squeak out words. "I—I just realized something." I paused to swallow the lump that was again making its way to my throat. I stood from the couch and paced around the living room to calm myself, although I'm not sure how much it helped. "The whole thing with Darla's boyfriend. It just doesn't make sense."

Savannah blinked like she wasn't sure what exactly I meant. At the same time, an expression crossed Collin's face that told me he was running through everything in his head.

I continued. "I mean, there's no mention of him in her phone anywhere. If she was going to run away with this guy, she must have loved him, right? Except that if that were true, she would have connected with him *somehow*. Collin, check her calls. Are there any incoming or outgoing calls to strange names or numbers?"

Collin quickly closed out the messaging app and opened the phone function and scrolled through it. His face fell. "No. It doesn't look like she made many calls."

I stopped pacing. "You see what I mean? She would have called him and talked to him for hours on end, don't you think? I mean, if she was close enough to him to want to run away."

Collin dropped his hands with the phone in them to his lap. "To be honest, I've been thinking the same thing."

"What? What is it?" Savannah's gaze shifted between the two of us.

I swallowed. "There is no mystery boyfriend."

The room went dead silent for what felt like a full minute, but it was probably only ten seconds.

When Savannah broke the silence, she spoke slowly. "Why did we even think there was a boyfriend in the first place?"

Collin ran his fingers through his hair and shifted uncomfortably. "Because it said it in the note she left."

I finally fell back down on the couch beside Collin. My leg heated in the spot that grazed against the side of his knee. "I don't get it," I finally said, twisting toward him. "Why would she say she was running away with some guy when she was going to meet up with this person?" I gestured to the phone. "Collin, what exactly did the note say?"

One hand came to rub his face as if he was trying to rid the tension from his expression. "I don't remember the exact words," he sighed. "It was something along the lines of, 'I'm sorry to do this to you again, but I love him and can't live without him anymore. You don't know him, but we're happy together.'" Collin paused like he was trying to remember the rest of the message. "Then it was something like, 'Don't worry about me. I love you both. Darla.'"

After a brief silence, Collin spoke again. "Sometimes I wonder if maybe my dad was trying to give her space like she asked. She said not to worry, but I just haven't been able to stop." His voice cracked before he could stop himself.

Savannah shook her head. "I don't get it. The note you just described and these texts don't match up. Do you think maybe she knew something was going to happen to her and was trying to save you and your dad the pain?"

Collin shook his head. "That doesn't make sense, either. If she thought she was in any real danger, she wouldn't have left the house."

I pressed my lips together in thought. Before I could say anything, Collin spoke again.

"I'm not sure we're asking the right question, though. I mean, I'm as interested as either of you to know what that letter meant and why Darla…I don't know…lied?" He said the word like it was a question, like he didn't know if it was the right word to use or if the statement was even true. "But these texts prove that she met someone at the bluff, where the rumors say she was murdered. If she met up with them, that'd make this person the murderer. So the question is, who is this mystery 'Traitor'?"

Savannah and I exchanged a *How should we know?* glance.

"The area code," Collin continued. "It's from around here, but I don't recognize the number. Do you think we can look it up or something?"

Savannah immediately had her phone out and began typing the number into a Google search. I eyed Darla's screen, where Collin had pulled up the texting conversation again. I didn't recognize the number, either, not that I expected to.

Savannah bit her lip while she scrolled through the search results. "Hmm…Right now I'm just seeing what

DISTANT DREAMS

carrier the number is on. I'm not sure we'll get an owner's name, though. I'll keep looking."

I realized for the first time that Google wasn't always as helpful as you wanted it to be. It was one thing to reverse look up landline phone numbers, but it was another to find the owner of a cell phone plan.

"Collin," I asked while Savannah fixated her attention on her phone, "do you have any theories?"

He pressed his lips together and shrugged. "It could be anyone, honestly." His eyes met mine. "Like I told you, she lost a lot of friends last year. Not all of them, but it could have been any of the ones who didn't stick around. Or it could have been someone else entirely."

Who could have done something so horrible to her that she would call them a traitor? A thought flickered through my mind, but I quickly shoved it away, only it resurfaced almost as quickly. *No*, I told myself. *It couldn't be her mother, could it*? I mean, her mom had abandoned her family, and that was enough to earn her "traitor" status, but what kind of mother would kill her own child? And why would her mom come back after so many years and ask to talk in private instead of meet her at home? No, that certainly didn't make sense. But who else would be a traitor in Darla's eyes?

"Can we take this to the police?" I asked.

Collin bit his bottom lip. "It doesn't prove much, does it? I mean, it proves she left the house that night, but not that she's dead."

185

I wasn't sure it was possible, but my heart sank even further into my chest.

"We should call the number," Savannah suggested.

"And say what?" I asked skeptically.

"It doesn't matter what you say. You just have to get a name." Savannah hopped up from my couch and grabbed the landline off its base and handed the phone to me. "Say you're from the local radio station. Say the number got entered into a drawing for concert tickets and you need their name to confirm their entry."

I spun the phone around in my hands, gazing at it warily. "You think that will work?"

Savannah nodded.

"But what about caller I.D.?" I asked.

"They won't know the difference," she promised.

"Here." I shoved the phone in her direction on the opposite side of Collin. "You do it. You're the actress."

She sighed and took the phone. Collin showed her the number on Darla's phone, and she began dialing.

I held my breath as the room went silent. All I could hear was the ringing phone on the other end of the line. When I heard a woman's voice, I began breathing again, but my breaths were shallow.

Savannah didn't say anything before she hung up the phone.

"What happened?" Collin asked.

"They didn't pick up," she answered.

"What do you mean?" My voice came out scratchy.

"It went to voicemail, and it was just an automated

message that repeated the number back to me. It sucks that the person didn't record their own message."

By now, I was starting to get a headache from the stress. "I guess we'll have to try again later." I rose from the couch and took the phone from Savannah's hand and set it back on its base. It was moments like this when I felt like giving up.

By the end of the night, we still didn't know who Darla's Traitor was, and I was beginning to think we wouldn't find anything to convince the police with. I crawled into bed that night more nervous than ever about what everything we'd just learned meant and where we would find the missing pieces.

19

I woke Friday morning alive with nerves. I'd once again dreamt about Darla, but that was nothing new.

To add to my stress, tonight was opening night for the play, and I had no idea how that would end. Would I miss a cue? Would I misplace a prop? I'd helped with Savannah's plays before, but I grew jittery every time an opening night came, and I wasn't even *in* the play. I couldn't imagine how the actors felt.

The school day passed like any other until lunchtime when Savannah left to meet up with Shawn. I was lucky enough that Collin caught my attention in the hall before I reached the cafeteria.

"Kai," he called from a few paces back.

My heart fluttered at the sound of his voice. "Yeah?" I twisted to face him as he closed the distance between us.

"Want to go off campus?"

I smiled and answered almost too quickly. "Sure!"

"Is Savannah around? Does she want to come, too?"

"She's already headed out with Shawn," I told him. "Do any of your friends want to tag along with us?"

Collin shook his head. "They drive for lunch."

"And you don't?" I asked while we walked.

He squinted into the sun as we exited the school. "Honestly, I like the walk more than the food, but the food isn't bad. The roast beef sandwiches are pretty good and not that terrible for you, either."

Collin and I found our way to a table outside of Amberg Hamburg after we ordered. I tried a roast beef sandwich since he recommended it. Our conversation remained casual, but as we got to talking more, I realized we had more in common than I ever thought. Sure, I'd known him since elementary school, but I never really *knew* him. Turns out his favorite movies were comedies, just like mine. He told me he preferred vanilla ice cream over chocolate—me, too—which resulted in the deal that we'd have to buy a gallon tub of vanilla ice cream sometime and share it. Collin even admitted to me that he was terrified of spiders. I wasn't exactly fond of them, either.

By the end of lunch, I was laughing hysterically at Collin while he tried, and continuously failed, to toss his garbage into the trash can two tables away. Each time it landed next to it, he'd run and pick it up before sitting back down in his seat to try again.

"You suck at this," I teased.

One of Collin's brows shot up. "You think you could do better?"

"I know I can," I assured him with a challenging stare.

"You think so?" he asked, handing me his balled up wrapper. "Let's see what you can do."

Uh oh. I spoke too soon. I pressed my lips together but couldn't refuse his challenge. "Please don't laugh," I begged as I tossed the wrapper. The shot was way to the left, but by some miracle, the wrapper bounced off the edge of the raised concrete flower bed alongside the dining area before reversing its course and landing square in the trash can.

My fists shot up in victory. "Yes!"

Collin raised his brows. "Maybe you should join the basketball team."

I snorted. "That was a lucky shot. I'd rather be on the cross country team or in track."

We both went silent after that, and an emotion I couldn't quite pinpoint knotted in my chest. If I wanted to run on a team, why didn't I? I could see in Collin's eyes that he was mentally asking the same question, but he didn't say anything.

"Maybe I'll go out for track," I finally said.

* * *

As the school day wore on, I thought more about

what I'd said to Collin. I really did miss being part of a team, and if I went out for track in the spring, I'd be running alongside Collin. It might be fun. But then again, what about saving up for traveling? Granted, I hadn't felt the urge to get away from Amberg as strong lately, but with my abilities to travel in my sleep gone, I *had* to travel someday to see everything I hadn't seen yet. To be fair, I had my whole life ahead of me to travel if I wanted to. I only had one cross country and two track seasons left. I could have fun with that now and work for a couple of years saving up for my big adventure after high school.

When I headed to the library for eighth period, I had decided to tell Collin I was set on joining track in the spring with him—that my travels could wait until my twenties—but when I walked into the library, he and Savannah were already chatting across the table at each other.

"No way," Savannah insisted. "Chocolate is way better than vanilla. I can't believe Kai has converted you to the dark side."

"Hey," I defended, sliding into a chair next to Collin. "If you ever noticed, chocolate is the dark one. You're the one on the dark side."

She rolled her eyes. "I suppose that sounds about right, but it's better over here on the dark side."

"Shouldn't you be working on your group project?" I accused lightheartedly.

She glanced toward the computers, where her two

group members were scrolling through a web page. "They don't seem to want my help at this point. I told them I'll put the slideshow together once we have all our research."

I eyed her skeptically while I opened my textbook. "Okay."

"What are you working on?" she asked, rising in her chair a bit to get a good look at my worksheet. "Math? I didn't understand question eight."

Collin glanced over at my paper to read the question. "Oh, that's simple. Kai, can I borrow your book?" I scooted it closer to him, and he flipped through a few pages before finding the lesson he was looking for. "Okay, it's on page eighty-seven. You use this equation here at the bottom of the page."

Savannah rose in her chair and leaned across the table to get a good look. Her pink shirt fell forward slightly to reveal even more cleavage than normal. I noticed Collin sneak a glance at her chest before averting his eyes like he was embarrassed for looking. Savannah inched closer for a better look at the page. The necklace charm Shawn had given her swayed back and forth like a pendulum.

Collin's eyes locked on her chest again. In the next moment, he drew in a sharp breath. "Where did you get that?" His gaze never dropped from the charm.

Savannah smiled proudly like she was glad he noticed her latest treasure. "My boyfriend gave it to me. Isn't it pretty?"

Collin didn't say anything for several seconds. I heard him swallow hard. And then my world stopped.

"I know who murdered my sister."

20

"*What?*" Savannah hissed in a low voice since we were in the library. She leaned back in her seat and pulled her necklace protectively to her chest.

Collin clenched his jaw. "That's my sister's necklace."

"What?" Savannah shook her head. "No, it's mine."

"You *are* dating Shawn Cameron, aren't you?"

Savannah nodded shyly. "And?"

"I swear that's the same necklace he gave my sister when they were dating."

My mouth hung open in shock. Could Shawn truly be the "Traitor" Darla had listed in her phone? He broke up with her, so it made sense, but how could we be sure? "Collin," I said, resting a hand on his shoulder to calm him down. "Are you sure? I mean, maybe he just likes the necklace and bought two of them."

"No," Collin insisted. "It's my sister's. She wore it all the time."

"On that night?" I asked skeptically, except the more I thought about it, the more Shawn fit into the picture. Maybe he wanted to meet up with her to talk about their breakup.

Collin thought about my question for a moment, and then his eyes lit up like he had a great idea. The next thing I knew, he was pulling out his phone right in the middle of the library and scrolling through it. A few moments later, he turned the screen to us. "Yes," he answered.

There on the screen was a photo of Darla on her Instagram page dressed for the homecoming dance. The necklace Savannah was currently wearing sparkled off Darla's chest.

My breath stopped. We found him. We found the killer. That's why Savannah needed a new necklace clasp, because it wasn't new.

"That doesn't make sense," Savannah insisted, but I couldn't miss the tears glistening in her eyes. Her arms crossed over her chest. "The number that texted her wasn't Shawn's."

My brow furrowed uncontrollably. "Are you sure? What if he got a new number recently?"

"The same night?" Savannah asked. "He gave me his number that same night. Besides, he was with me."

I let that sink in for a moment before I realized

something. "Didn't you say he left the party earlier than you?"

Savannah glanced around nervously. "I—I guess so."

"He didn't say where he was going?" Collin asked.

"We weren't really 'together' then," she admitted. "He didn't exactly confide in me."

Uh oh. This was starting to make too much sense. Shawn didn't have an alibi. I could see it in Savannah's eyes that she was starting to wonder if our suspicions were true.

"Well, he doesn't exactly talk fondly of her," she admitted. "But he didn't do it. I would know. He's my boyfriend."

"Of two weeks," Collin pointed out.

"What does that matter?" Savannah raised her voice.

"Hey," Collin bit back but still quietly enough that he wouldn't get reprimanded by the librarian. "You suspected *me*. Can't we just entertain the idea of your boyfriend for a second?"

Savannah glanced at me accusingly like she knew I'd told Collin about her suspicions, except I didn't. I'd only confirmed them.

"Fine," she finally said, probably because she felt bad for suspecting Collin and this was her way of easing her guilt for it. "You two can entertain the idea, but I'm not going to listen to it." She shot up from her chair dramatically.

"How well do you really know him?" Collin called after her as she rushed off to the computers to find her project group. She just kept walking like she didn't hear him, but I noticed a semi-pause in her step when he asked the question.

My heart broke a little as I watched her walk away. I wanted to chase after her, to explain how it all made sense, but as soon as she scooted a chair next to her group, she shot me a glare that said, *Don't you dare.*

I bit my lower lip and turned to Collin. "I'm scared," I admitted in a low whisper.

He surprised me when his fingers closed the distance between our hands to hold mine under the table. "There's nothing to be scared of. We got him."

I shook my head and looked down at our hands. "Not really." My voice cracked. "I mean, there's no way to prove that necklace is the same one, is there? We could go to the police with our theory, but they'll continue to insist she only ran away and is free to go as she pleases and all of that."

Collin pressed his lips together in thought. "You're right, but I don't know what else to do."

I was coming to the same conclusion. If it was Shawn, then we had to turn him in. I couldn't stand by and let Savannah continue hanging out with him when she could be his next victim. Then again, what if it wasn't Shawn? What if we turned him in and he had nothing to do with it and the necklace was just another one like Darla's?

My head ached as all these thoughts raced through it. I pressed my fingers to my temples to ease the tension. "It wouldn't be fair to turn him in without proof, without being one hundred percent sure. And it's not like anyone will believe us without evidence anyway." I sighed, dropping my shoulders.

"We have proof," Collin whispered, glancing back at Savannah. "Shawn had my sister's necklace."

"Well, it's not like Savannah is just going to let us *take* it," I pointed out. "She's a good friend, but she's also stubborn. We need something else."

"Like what?"

"Like a—" I paused in search of the answer. "A confession."

Collin snorted. "And how are we going to squeeze that out of him? He'd only tell someone he trusts."

My eyes fell on Savannah across the library as Collin spoke, and that's when my idea struck.

* * *

I cornered Savannah at her locker after the last bell rang.

"I'm not mad at you," she said without looking at me.

Oh, really? You have a good way of showing it, I thought, but instead I just said, "Oh?"

She turned to me. Most of the students had already fled the halls for the day. "Am I upset? Yeah. But you're still my best friend. I did the same thing to you by accusing Collin."

"So, we're good?"

Savannah nodded. "We're good, as long as you realize my boyfriend had nothing to do with this," she insisted stubbornly.

"But Savannah—" I started, but she cut me off.

"Look, I have plans to hang out with Shawn before I have to be in the auditorium for makeup. I know he didn't do it, so don't try to stop me." She slammed her locker and began walking, and I fell into step beside her. Something in her tone left me uncertain of her words, like she was just saying them to convince herself.

"That's perfect," I told her.

She eyed me skeptically.

"I mean, Collin and I came up with this idea. I think it will satisfy all of our curiosity, but we need your help."

She stopped in her tracks and turned to me. Tears brimmed in her eyes. "I—I don't want to."

"But Savannah, you could prove us wrong."

She dropped her head. "That's not what I'm afraid of." Her voice cracked. "I'm scared that you might be right."

So she really was just lying to herself. The tears in her eyes let go, and I pulled her into a hug, thankful that there were no longer any other students roaming the halls.

I eventually drew away from her and looked her straight in the eyes while gripping her shoulders.

"Savannah, it's going to be okay. If we do this, we'll know what really happened. At least, I hope so."

She wiped the tears from her eyes and sniffled. "What would I have to do?"

"We need your acting skills."

Her eyes lit up slightly before dimming to normal. "You mean, I have to lie to my boyfriend?"

I shook my head. "Not exactly. We were thinking that if he trusted you, you may be able to get a confession out of him. We'd be there hiding with a camera. It'd be three against one, so you'd be safe."

The halls grew eerily quiet as I waited for Savannah's response. We stood there for so long that I was almost sure Collin had already left the meeting spot we agreed upon. I swallowed hard when she opened her mouth. I thought I was sure of what she'd say, so I was surprised when something else entirely came out.

"Okay. We can try it."

21

A few minutes later, we entered the commons. I breathed a sigh of relief when I saw Collin was still there waiting for us.

"She's going to help." I spoke in a soft whisper as I approached him.

"Thanks, Savannah," Collin said shyly before meeting her eyes. "It means a lot."

Savannah simply nodded. She stole a glance at her phone before finally speaking. "I was supposed to meet Shawn five minutes ago. We agreed to grab some French fries at Amberg Hamburg before the play. I'm supposed to meet him by the gym doors. Do you think it's safe to go alone?"

"Don't worry. You won't be alone," Collin assured her. "We'll be right behind you. We can sit a table over from you while you talk. We'll be recording the whole time."

Savannah bit her lip nervously. "Let's just say for a second…" She paused. "If he did do it, then he wouldn't just admit it in front of a group of people. How about I try to…I don't know…lure him somewhere more private?"

"No one usually sits outside," I pointed out. "We could hide behind the raised flower bed and record."

"How will I convince him to tell me the truth?" she asked.

I rested a hand on her shoulder. "Savannah, you're an amazing actress. I've seen you improv like nobody's business. And your poker face? Flawless. You can do this."

After a second, she nodded confidently. "Okay, you're right." She began walking in the direction of the gym, where she was supposed to meet up with Shawn. "I just hope you're wrong about him."

Collin and I kept our distance but stayed close enough to Savannah and Shawn that we could see them and respond quickly if anything went wrong. Luckily, Shawn never looked back to notice us following him. I watched Savannah slip her hand into his and lean on his arm as they walked, which left a bad taste in my mouth. If anyone else had witnessed the couple chatting on their walk, everything would appear normal. Heck, even Shawn probably thought everything was fine considering how good of an actress I knew Savannah was. She threw her head back and laughed at something he said, but inside, she was probably just as nervous and frightened as I was.

When they entered the doors of Amberg Hamburg, true fear finally took over. My mouth went dry, and my hands began shaking. I knew Shawn wouldn't do anything to my best friend in public, but having her out of my sight frightened me in a way I couldn't control. Collin surprised me by grabbing my hand for a second time that day. My eyes flew to his, though his touch eased my nerves.

"It's going to be okay," he told me in such a soothing voice that I couldn't help but believe him.

We found our way behind the flower bed that separated the outdoor seating area from the sidewalk. "Are you ready?" I asked nervously while pulling my sweatshirt sleeves over my fists to keep them warm.

Collin lowered the volume on his phone to silent and then opened the camera application. "Yep."

I didn't know what Savannah said to get Shawn to eat outside when there was still plenty of seating indoors, but they emerged from the building a few minutes later and found their way to the table nearest us. There wasn't anyone else around.

When Collin and I secretly snuck a peek through the thick mums, I noticed that Savannah was smart enough to sit facing us so that Shawn sat across from her with his back to us. Collin began recording.

"Shawn," Savannah started. Her voice was plenty

loud enough for us to hear clearly and pick up on the camera.

"Yeah?" he asked in a melodic voice. No wonder he was a lady killer. Even his voice made a girl's ovaries perk up. Well, except for mine, because I knew what he had done. Shawn bit into a fry while Savannah spoke.

"I was wondering if I could ask you something."

I held my breath. She wasn't going to just come out and say it, was she?

"Anything, baby," Shawn said before shoving another ketchup-covered fry in his face.

"Well, we've been dating for a couple of weeks now, and, well…" She tucked a strand of brown hair behind her ear and pulled her bottom lip into her mouth seductively. "I've never…" She cleared her throat. "I've never *been* with anyone."

Even from the back, I could see that Shawn had stopped chewing mid-bite. I could only imagine what kind of expression was fixed on his face at that moment.

"You're kidding," he said in disbelief.

Savannah batted her eyes at him in a way that he wouldn't have noticed unless he knew her as well as I did. "I'm serious, and I thought that…maybe…maybe you'd like to be my first."

I swear I saw the breath leave Shawn's chest. I wasn't sure where Savannah was going with this, but I could tell it was going to be good, offering him something he couldn't refuse before dropping the bomb.

Shawn reached across the table to rest his hand on Savannah's. "You sure, baby? The other day you said you weren't ready."

"Well," she swallowed, "I changed my mind. I'm ready now."

Shawn ran his fingers through his hair. "That's...wow. You know I really like you, right?"

Savannah maintained her sweet, innocent girl act. "I like you too, Shawn."

"So, like, when? Now?" His voice was full of too much hope, which made me want to hurl.

"If you think there's enough time."

"Oh, baby. Don't worry. There's enough time."

Sick! I thought. Collin and I exchanged a look of disgust before fixing our eyes back on the scene playing out before us.

Savannah rolled her necklace around in her fingers. "The thing is, I want to know that I can trust you completely. I just—I always told myself that whoever I lost it to, I'd trust with all my heart, that I'd love them."

"You can trust me, baby. I promise."

Savannah nodded, and a somber expression crossed her face. If I didn't know she was acting, I would have fallen for this whole conversation, too. "Then will you answer a question for me?"

Shawn nodded, almost too eagerly. "Of course. What is it, baby?"

Savannah paused for dramatic effect. "Where'd you buy me this necklace?"

Shawn shifted uncomfortably while my own fingers grasped on tighter to the corner of the flower bed. "Why do you ask?"

She paused. "Never mind. It's silly, really." Knowing Savannah the way I did, I could tell these words were calculated for effect.

"Come on, you can tell me. Why are you interested?"

"I just had this silly idea. Like I said, it's really stupid." She averted her gaze from his.

"Savannah," Shawn said firmly like he was honestly concerned for her. "What's wrong?"

"Well, I know it's stupid, but I was looking through your Facebook page."

"And?" I could practically hear Shawn raise his eyebrows.

Savannah spoke slowly. "I was just interested, and I saw a picture. There was one of you and Darla together when you were dating. She was wearing this same necklace."

Shawn tensed ever so slightly, but his tone was firm. "Savannah, what's your real question?"

She swallowed to clear her throat before spitting out her words. "Did you buy this necklace for me or for your ex-girlfriend?"

"I—" Shawn appeared at a loss of words.

Oh, what I would give to see the look on his face at this moment. I inched closer to Collin to get a better look through the flowers until the edge of my leg just barely touched his.

"Please be honest with me, Shawn," Savannah said sweetly. "I just want to know I can trust you."

Shawn visibly relaxed like he just remembered her offer. The sigh he gave seemed to stretch on for minutes as I wondered what he could possibly say next. Was there a reasonable explanation? Would he lie? What was the truth, anyway?

After a long silence like Shawn was calculating the costs and benefits, he finally spoke. "Okay, Savannah. I'll tell you the truth."

My pulse quickened, and so did Collin's breath beside me.

"I admit I bought the necklace for Darla, but you have to understand that it was really expensive. It's not just some cheap knock-off from the clearance rack at Wal-Mart. The truth is, I got the necklace back from her because really, it was mine, and I wanted you to have it. You're my girl now."

That's when Savannah broke down. The façade she'd just put on crumbled around her. Her hand slapped to her mouth, and her shoulders began shaking uncontrollably.

"Savannah, what's wrong?" Shawn asked in a tone that said he actually cared, one you wouldn't think would come out of a heartless murderer.

"It's true," Savannah cried, staring into Shawn's face in horror.

"Hey," he said sympathetically. "I'm sorry. We can

get you another one, one that's just yours." Shawn reached across the table for Savannah's hand, but she immediately recoiled.

"I don't care about the necklace!" She sprang to her feet.

"Then what's going on?" Shawn's voice rose like Savannah's.

"You don't get it, do you?"

"Savannah, it's just a necklace."

"This isn't about the necklace, Shawn." She slowly took a step back without distancing herself too far. Luckily, Shawn didn't advance. "I saw another picture, okay? It was the night of the homecoming dance, and Darla was wearing *this* necklace." Tears began streaming down her face now. "That was the night Darla disappeared. You left the party early."

"Oh, my God," Shawn said slowly, rising from his chair ever so slightly. "You think—"

Savannah interrupted before he had a chance to speak. The tension growing in the air sent a nervous shudder through my body. "Darla didn't run away, did she, Shawn?"

"Savannah," he said firmly, extending a hand out to her like he was trying to reason with a rabid dog. "Calm down, please. I'll explain everything."

"How you—" her voice caught in her throat. She lowered her voice to a whisper. "How you killed your ex-girlfriend?"

"Please, Savannah," he begged. "Please just sit

down. I'll explain everything. I swear to you I didn't kill her."

Something in his voice seemed to reassure Savannah because a moment later, she was slowly easing into the seat across from him. By now, my heart felt like it was trying to beat its way out of my chest, and I could sense Collin nervously shivering from beside me. Without thinking, I reached for Collin's bicep and leaned into him. I needed the comfort to calm my nerves. He didn't seem to notice, but if he did, he didn't mind.

Savannah spoke in such a quiet voice that I'm not sure the camera could even pick it up, yet her tone seemed so even and controlled, like she owned the situation. Her palms lay firmly on the table in front of her, and a dark look crossed her eyes. "Shawn, do you know what happened to Darla?"

After a long pause, he spoke with a wavering tone. "Yes."

A pained expression crossed Savannah's face when she gulped, making it look like she was swallowing needles. "Is she dead?"

He paused for a second time, and when he answered, his voice cracked like he was holding back tears. "Yes."

Savannah's eyes shifted, but she maintained a controlled tone that she seemed to pull out of nowhere. "Did you kill her?"

"No," Shawn answered in a near whisper.

"Do you know who did?"

Shawn couldn't answer audibly this time. Instead, he nodded his head as if he was ashamed of the answer.

"Who?" Savannah asked warily, setting off the last bomb in a string of attacks.

In the next few moments, time seemed to stand still. My breath ceased, Collin froze next to me, and even the sounds of the wind seemed to die off. Then, Shawn spoke the name that would change the course of our entire investigation.

"Tiana King."

22

"I—I have to go." Savannah stood.

"Savannah, please," Shawn cried.

She whirled around toward him before I could truly process the name Shawn had just given us.

"No, Shawn!" Savannah insisted.

He stopped in his tracks when she faced him with a hard look. Collin and I remained paralyzed in place, continuing to watch the scene unfold as we hoped more information would surface. We couldn't break in now, not when the confessions were only beginning to roll.

"How do you know all that?" Savannah demanded. "You may not have killed her, but you..." She broke into sobs again. "You left the party early. You—"

"I'm sorry, Savannah. I know what I did was wrong, and I feel awful for it now, but I can't turn Tiana in. I'm an accessory."

"What the hell does that mean?" Savannah's voice rose without either of them moving.

Shawn ran his fingers through his hair vigorously. "Look, Tiana and I are friends. I was the one person she trusted. When—after it happened, she called me, okay? I hate myself for what I did, but I helped her. I helped her cover it up. That's when I took the necklace. "

"Why?" Savannah asked in a small voice. "Why would you help her?"

"It was an accident," Shawn insisted. "If anyone finds out, it will ruin Tiana's life. Darla was already gone, and there was nothing we could do. I was just helping out a friend, okay?"

All of this was beginning to make sense now. The mystery number must have been Tiana's. She had told me she and Darla weren't friends anymore. She had dated Shawn as soon as he and Darla broke up. She definitely fit the "Traitor" category. Then there was that time at rehearsal when I witnessed Tiana tell Shawn she "owned" him. This must have been what she was talking about. If he helped her, it meant she had something on him, and for as long as they were the only people who knew, she had complete control over him.

"Please don't tell anyone," Shawn begged. "It was an accident."

I had to hold back from scoffing. Smashing someone over the head with a rock was no accident.

"Look," Savannah said. "I'm glad you told me, but

I just don't think I can be around you right now."

"But I was honest with you, Savannah," he said like that would make it all better.

"Just don't, Shawn. I won't tell anyone, okay? But I just need some time to think."

"You won't?" He sounded surprised.

"I won't, but there are already rumors of her death. It's only a matter of time…"

"Those are just stupid rumors," Shawn insisted. "I heard them, and they're not based on truth. It was just someone making up theories for why she hasn't been in school. I admit, I was scared at first, but no one is going to find out. I'm not a bad guy, Savannah, and if we can keep this secret, we can be together."

"Please," Savannah begged. "Just give me time."

Shawn nodded. "Yeah, okay. I can do that."

Savannah turned and hurried off into the building. I tensed as she disappeared, knowing right now that neither Collin nor I could move or Shawn would see us. He returned to his table to grab his trash and then tossed it into the garbage near us, much too close for my liking. Then he headed off in the opposite direction, probably back to the school to get his car.

I breathed a sigh of relief, which felt like my first breath in the last half hour or so. I lowered myself from the edge of the flower bed and twisted to rest my back against the cold concrete. Collin turned off his recording and knelt next to me.

"You okay?" he asked.

I thought about the question for a long time before finally nodding. Honestly, that couldn't have gone better. We finally had something to convince people with and bring Darla's killer to justice.

"Let's go inside," I suggested breathlessly, gesturing to the door.

Collin nodded and grabbed my hand to pull me up from the ground. We found Savannah seated in a corner table. Her eyes were still bloodshot from tears.

"Hey, Savannah," I said sympathetically as I slid into a seat at her table. "I'm sorry."

"No, it's okay," she told me, but even with her great acting skills, I could tell it wasn't okay.

"You were right," I pointed out. "It wasn't Shawn. I'm sorry about the way we made you feel."

Collin pulled out a chair next to me and sat in it.

"No," Savannah insisted. "You were right. Shawn is dangerous, and it was stupid of me not to listen to you. I'm glad we did this. I needed to know the truth."

"We all did," Collin said, "and now so can everyone."

"Hey, Savannah." I gave an encouraging smile, but she didn't meet my gaze. "It's going to be okay."

She finally raised her eyes to look at me. "You're probably right. Hey," she said, her discontent fading mildly. "Maybe I can play Cinderella now that our lead is a criminal." The joke wasn't admittedly one of Savannah's best moments, but it helped cheer her up ever so slightly, and we managed to get her out of her seat.

"What now?" I asked when we escaped into the autumn air.

"We go turn the bitch in," Collin said. His language caught me slightly off guard.

"Do you have a car?" Savannah asked him.

He shook his head. "It's at home. I like walking to school."

"Us, too," I said disappointedly. "I guess we're going to have to walk."

Savannah caught my attention before we started toward the station. "Sorry, Kai. I meant what I said. I have a lot to think about, and I'm not going to talk to anyone about this, at least not now. I don't want to go to the police station with you."

I swallowed the disappointment rising in my throat. I couldn't say I understood why she chose to promise that to Shawn, but I respected her decision to keep her promise.

"Okay," I agreed after a few seconds. "We'll walk you home, I guess."

"Actually," she said, "can you walk me back to the school? Lindsay and Tyler should be there, so I'll be safe with them until you're done at the police station. I want to be with the cast when they hear. They're my...well, they're my team. I have to be there for them."

I agreed, and we walked Savannah back to the school. Just like she predicted, we found Mr. Spears, Tyler, and Lindsay in the auditorium. Savannah put on a smile to mask her emotions and rushed off to join Tyler for conversation.

"Ready?" Collin asked. His beautiful brown eyes stared into mine.

I nodded nervously. I just wanted this to all be over. We fell into step side-by-side, and I slipped my hand into Collin's. I half-expected him to pull away, to say he didn't like me like that, but instead, he squeezed my hand for courage, which helped slightly.

It was a longer walk to the police station than I had anticipated. I took a deep breath before reaching for the door. I pulled. It didn't budge. All I could do was stand there in shock for a second before pulling at the door again.

"What the...?" I released Collin's grip and stepped back from the door. That's when I noticed the hours of operation. They were only open until 4:00.

Collin checked his phone for the time. "Dang it. We missed them. What do we do now?" His eyes locked onto mine like I should have all the answers.

My mouth hung open without replying. I didn't know.

"Where do you find a cop when they're not at the police station?" Collin asked, almost in desperation.

"I don't know. At their houses, like everyone else when they're not at work." That came out too snarky. I took another breath to calm myself. Then something in my mind clicked. "Wait. There's Jack."

"And?" Collin asked curiously.

"Jack is my mom's friend, and he's a police officer. Maybe if we can find him, he can help."

"Where do we find him?"

My eyes shifted in thought, not really focusing on anything. If it was later in the night, I'd say he'd be at my house hanging out with my mom, but my mom wouldn't be home from work yet, so he obviously wouldn't be there without her. Unfortunately for us, as long as I'd known Jack, I never had a desire to visit him at his home. I had no idea where he lived.

"I don't know—" I started, but I quickly changed course when I realized something. "Wait. Jack told me he'd be at the play for opening night tonight. We could find him in the crowd before the play starts, and you can give him the video."

Collin nodded slowly. "Are you sure he'll be there?"

"Well, he told me he would be. I'm not fond of the guy, but he's honest. He's not the kind of guy who just says things like that, so yeah, he'll be there."

Collin scratched the side of his face and then sighed. "Okay, yeah. I guess we can do that."

"Okay, well, let's break a leg."

23

I decided it was best to go through the motions and pretend everything was normal, but the next two hours of makeup and stage prep seemed to tick by at an unusually slow pace. I peeked my head through the curtain several times, hoping that by some miracle Jack had shown up early for some reason. He didn't. I filled in Savannah about our plan in whispers while she reluctantly applied the makeup she probably wouldn't need.

"They were closed," I told her, careful not to say too much in case someone overheard. Tiana wasn't anywhere in sight, but there were other girls nearby who might overhear. "Jack said he was coming tonight. We figured we could talk to him then."

Savannah swallowed nervously like she was

honestly afraid about what was going to happen. I had never seen her scared like this before. "Can I talk to you for a second?" she whispered. She glanced around before grabbing my arm and pulling me into the privacy of the hallway.

"Yeah?" I asked, still whispering.

She knotted her fingers together and stared down at her hands nervously. "What do you think is going to happen?"

"Um…Tiana is going to jail," I said like it was obvious.

"No, I mean, will Jack arrest her on stage or something?"

I hadn't thought that through yet, though I'd briefly wondered the same thing myself. After all, Tiana *was* the lead. We'd ruin the whole play by telling Jack beforehand. But at the same time, it was the right thing to do.

"Savannah, she's dangerous. She deserves whatever she gets."

"I agree with you. But—this is really selfish, I know." She took a deep breath like she couldn't believe she was suggesting this. "Can Jack maybe wait until the play is over tonight? It's just, we charge admission, and it helps the drama club. If he arrests her before the play, we'll have to refund everyone their admission."

A silence fell over the hallway before Savannah spoke again, changing her mind. "No, that's stupid. It's selfish. You're right. She deserves what she gets, and she should get it as soon as possible. She's already been running around for two weeks with no consequences."

Savannah hung her head, and I understood immediately how important the drama department was to her. If they lost the income they'd earn from opening night, the club would be devastated and wouldn't have enough money to run their play in the spring.

I rested a hand on her shoulder, which got her to look at me. "I'll see what I can do. But you know this means the drama club only gets money from tonight, right? You'll hardly break even."

Savannah nodded shamefully, guilty for her selfishness, yet I felt for her. The plays were the one thing she had, and if she lost the spring play, that'd be one less chance to be cast as the lead.

She gave a forced smile. "Thanks, but at least with opening night, we'll earn enough back that we can make up the rest with fundraising."

"I'll talk to Collin," I promised her.

I escaped to the stage and stuck my head through the curtains again. Collin sat in the front row and fidgeted nervously while he waited. Several other groups of students who had come in with other cast and crew members scattered the auditorium seats. My eyes bore into him, willing him to look up. Finally, he gazed in my direction. I signaled to him to meet me in the hall next to the stage.

"What's up?" Collin asked nervously when we met.

"I just talked to Savannah," I told him a low

whisper. "I know how wrong this sounds, but she was hoping that Jack won't take any action until after curtain call. The drama club really needs the income from opening night. It's their biggest night."

"Kai," Collin said firmly but softly, a combination I didn't think possible. "This is—" He looked around to make sure no one was nearby and then lowered his voice. "This is my sister's *murderer* we're talking about."

I hung my head. "I know, but they just need this one night. If the main character is gone, they'll have to refund everyone. I know how it sounds, but..." I trailed off as I met his eyes. A look of hurt and desperation filled them. Like Savannah, I changed my mind when I heard myself try to reason the situation. "I'm sorry. It's not right. You should do whatever you want. She deserves to rot in jail."

"This is really important to you, isn't it?" he asked softly.

I nodded. "Well, it's important to Savannah. But—"

Collin gripped my shoulders to pull my attention back to his face after I'd looked away. His eyes shifted between mine, like he saw my pain and was sympathizing with me. "Okay."

"Savannah said that if they get the admission for opening night, they can do some fundraising and still have enough for the spring play." I spoke too quickly for my own liking.

"I said okay."

Oh. I hadn't realized what he'd meant before. Apparently he changed his mind as well. Collin continued. "It's not just about me. It's about you and Savannah and the whole drama department."

"Thank you," I told him, truly grateful that he was so understanding. Before I knew what I was doing, I'd planted a kiss on his cheek and was headed back to the girls' dressing room. It was only two seconds later on my way down the hall that I realized what I'd just done by kissing him. A grin spread across my face, but I couldn't work up the courage to look back at him.

The prep work proceeded as normal, though now that I knew what Tiana had done, I only grew annoyed the more she talked. Her voice rose above everyone else's in the room, and it made my skin crawl. I couldn't believe what I was doing by postponing her arrest.

Savannah felt the same way. "Gawd, she needs to shut up about now," she complained to me in a whisper.

Honestly, her presence gave me shivers, but I plastered an expression of courage on my face, and it seemed to work. I had to act normal.

"Maybe I should go find Jack," I told Savannah, having second thoughts.

"Please don't just yet. We need this night for drama club." I could hear the regret in Savannah's tone, like she wasn't quite sure if this was a good idea, either.

It didn't really matter at this point because the play was just minutes from starting. We couldn't back out of our decision now.

I spent the next hour and a half sitting in the girls' dressing room with Lindsay while we waited for set changes. The door remained propped open when no one was changing so that we could hear the lines—otherwise we wouldn't be able to spot our cues. At various intervals, we escaped onto the stage to change the sets. A few times, I had to help people into their costumes, but mostly it was a lot of sitting around.

I noticed my breath grow increasingly hotter each time I heard Tiana's voice over the speakers. Toward the end of the second act, I saw Lindsay gritting her teeth the same time I frustratingly pressed my lips together in response to the way Tiana spoke one of her lines, like she was queen or something—although I guess playing a princess, she wasn't far off from that.

"What is it?" I asked Lindsay.

She sighed. The other actors were either on stage, in the hallway waiting for their cues, or sitting in the greenroom, so we were alone. "Tiana," Lindsay admitted. "She just…she gets on my nerves."

"Doesn't she get on everyone's?" I joked. Oh, how I wanted to tell Lindsay so badly that she wouldn't have to worry about Tiana in a couple of hours, once I told Jack the truth, but I kept my lips sealed.

"Pretty much," Lindsay agreed.

We both went silent for a beat, and then I heard the quick patter of feet down the hall, a step I recognized and now feared. Lindsay noticed as well, which quickly shut the both of us up. In the next moment, Tiana burst into the dressing room in a rage. She had completed her scene, and her mic was turned off. When she stormed past the door, she kicked the doorstop out of the way, leaving the door to fall shut with a click so that Lindsay and I were the only ones to witness the scene. We both stood in surprise.

"What the fuck, Lindsay?" Tiana spat. She held her peasant skirt up by both hands.

Lindsay was too timid to reply, but I could see the fear in her eyes when I glanced at her.

With Lindsay frozen like she was, I managed to work up enough courage to speak up. "What's wrong, Tiana?" I asked in the kindest voice I could manage.

"She," Tiana snarled, pointing a finger toward Lindsay, "didn't fix my costume like I told her to! Two buttons fell off on stage, and my skirt practically slipped off! I had to improvise and hold it up the entire last scene."

My throat closed up. Crap. I recognized Tiana's skirt. It was the one Lindsay had made me help fix. I'd told Lindsay I didn't know how to sew buttons, and I must have not secured them properly, or I tied the knot wrong or something. And here Tiana was chewing out Lindsay when it was my fault.

"Tiana, I'm sorry—" I started, but she cut me off.

"Stay out of this. It's not about you. It's about this incompetent *girl* who thinks she has skill but is really just useless. You don't act, Lindsay, because you can't. So you sit in the background sewing costumes, only—

oops—you can't do that, either."

None of us moved from our positions, but I stole a glance over at Lindsay and noticed the tears welling up in her eyes. She knew I was the one who sewed on those buttons, yet she was taking the blame. I couldn't let her do that.

"Tiana, it wasn't Linds—"

"I told you to stay out of it. Thankfully, I only have to wear this costume for one more scene." She crossed the room to the counter, where most girls had left their makeup bags. "Now, I know someone must have a safety pin or two."

"Hey!" I called, but I didn't move from the spot where my feet were grounded. "You can't just go through people's stuff!" Except that's exactly what she was doing.

"Well, I can't exactly go on stage with a broken costume, can I?" she countered. By some miracle, she quickly found a safety pin and held it up triumphantly. "Help," she demanded, staring me in the eyes. I had no choice but to comply. "Don't forget about the last costume change," she told me in a not so friendly manner before heading back out of the room.

The door fell shut, leaving Lindsay and me alone. For the first time since Tiana had stormed in here, Lindsay made a sound.

I immediately rushed to her side to console her as she lowered herself back into her chair. "Hey, it's okay. She didn't mean it. I'm the one to blame." Except the problem was that it sounded like Tiana believed every word she'd said about Lindsay. It made my blood boil. I was ready to give that bitch what she deserved at this point, play cancelled and refunds given or not.

Lindsay raised her head. "She's right. I'm a terrible actress. That's why I don't act. And the costumes? Who am I kidding?"

I ground my teeth together. I may not have known Lindsay well, but she was my friend, and she did not deserve to feel this way. "That's not true, Lindsay. You're great at costumes." I paused and took a seat beside her. The surface of my skin burned in anger.

A single tear fell down Lindsay's cheek, and that's when I snapped.

"Don't worry," I told Lindsay. "She's going to get what's coming to her."

24

I clenched my fists as I pushed my way out of the dressing room and toward the sound booth, where Tyler was running the lights and mics. Tiana's attack on Lindsay had ignited the anger I'd been holding back. She deserved whatever she got.

I kept my voice low when I met Tyler because the play was still going on. One of his friends who'd volunteered to help sat nearby.

"Hey," I greeted in a whisper.

"Hey," Tyler said back, pushing his long black hair out of his eyes. "What's up?"

"After curtain call, turn Tiana's mic back on."

He furrowed his brow. "What? Everyone will be leaving by then."

"I know."

"Then what's going on?"

"Trust me," I assured him. "You're going to want to leave her mic on."

Tyler's gaze darted to Tiana on stage, and then his lips curled up mischievously. He had no idea what was going on, but I could tell he knew I was cooking up a dirty little plan. Clearly, he wasn't a fan of her, either.

"And I suppose you're not going to tell me," he accused.

"No, but trust me, it's going to be good."

"Okay," he agreed.

I hurried back to the dressing room, where I was needed in only a few minutes. I pulled Tiana's Cinderella ball gown off the hanger and unzipped it, getting ready for her after curtain call.

Lindsay noticed. "I'm going to go wait in the hall," she told me while eying the dress. I didn't blame her for not wanting to face Tiana again.

"That's probably a good idea," I told her before she pushed open the door and exited the room.

A few minutes later, Tiana entered. We were alone because all the other actors were already headed out for the receiving line. We were supposed to do this in under a minute so she could get out there, too.

"Quick, help me," she demanded. She turned around so I could undo the safety pin on her skirt.

I laid the ball gown I was holding across one of the chairs so I could help her.

Tiana unclipped her microphone and set it on the

counter while I fumbled with the safety pin. "Hurry up," she insisted.

My fingers quivered unintentionally. *I can do this*, I told myself. It wasn't so hard to work up the courage when just the sight of her made me want to punch her in the face. But I wasn't exactly a boxer or anything, so I'd have to fight with my words.

"Tiana." I spoke with a small voice. "Can I ask you something?"

"Make it snappy."

I tossed the safety pin onto the counter to my right and turned to grab the dress. Tiana had already stripped off her skirt and was working on her top.

"How did it feel—" I paused for a second as my throat closed up around my words. Could I really do this? My eyes drifted to the microphone resting on the counter, and that sent a bout of confidence through me. Not only could I do this, but I *had* to do it. No doubt everyone was already listening. Luckily, we couldn't hear anything through the closed door.

"How did what feel?" she asked, gesturing for me to help her into the dress. "Opening night? It was good."

"No, that's not what I meant." I pulled the dress up around her body and began zipping the back, making sure to pull the fabric aside at the trouble spot she'd shown me. "I meant, how did it feel to murder your best friend?" I finished the sentence just as I pulled the zipper up all the way.

She whirled around, her nostrils flaring. "What the

fuck? Who told you that?"

"There are rumors," I said confidently.

Tiana rolled her eyes. "Those are just rumors. Everyone knows Darla ran away. Now, if you'll excuse me."

She began pushing past me, but I stopped her by planting my body between hers and the door. My pulse quickened, and I couldn't believe how brave I was being. Tiana pursed her lips and crossed her arms over her chest.

My voice came out stronger than I felt. "So, you're saying you didn't smash a rock over Darla Baxter's head the night of the homecoming dance?"

Tiana's mouth hung open, and her eyes widened. I knew I had her.

"Whatever you heard, you're wrong," she insisted.

"You mean, you weren't up on the bluff that night? You didn't text Darla asking her to meet you there? Your number isn't listed as 'Traitor' in her phone?" My hands shook nervously, but I didn't let the uncertainty show in my voice.

Tiana took a step back to distance herself from me, and her arms fell to her sides. The fear in her eyes made it look like *she* was scared of *me*. "How do you know all that?"

"So, you're not denying it? Why'd you do it, Tiana?" My voice rose slightly, which helped steadying my hands. "What was it? You had already stolen her boyfriend. You turned half her friends against her.

What, you couldn't handle that after all of that she still made it on the homecoming court?"

"Oh, my God. No!"

"So, what? She said she had a boyfriend. Maybe you couldn't handle that someone was interested in her when no one would date you."

"No! It wasn't that at all! It was an accident!" Tiana's eyes widened further—though I didn't think that was possible. Her hands flew over her mouth like she'd just realized what she said. She'd just confessed.

"Why, then?" I demanded, my voice still loud. I still only half believed she had actually admitted to it.

Tiana retreated slowly until the back of her knees hit a chair. She sank down into it, perhaps realizing that making it to the receiving line by now was useless.

"I swear to God that I didn't mean to do it," she started in a near whisper. "It was an accident. I *swear*."

"Tiana, what happened?" I asked for my own curiosity and for those who were in the auditorium listening to her confession. I just hoped Tyler had remembered to turn her mic back on.

"It was all about homecoming," she admitted, not meeting my gaze. "I'm a bitch, okay? I always have been." She forced a laugh like she found that amusing, and then she continued slowly. "I liked Shawn, and I wanted him for myself. I had been trying to get them to break up for months, and when I saw my opportunity at the homecoming after party last year, I took it."

I swallowed, not daring to move for fear that she'd

break out of the spell that put her in confession mode.

"I was supposed to find the homecoming queen and blindfold her so she could go do the stupid Seven Minutes in Heaven thing. I found Darla first and blindfolded her. I came up from behind, so she never knew it was me, and she just went along with it at first because she was so wasted. No one noticed because blindfolded, she looked like the homecoming queen. They were even wearing the same dress. It was such a perfect plot.

"Anyway, I put her in the closet knowing that Shawn would get mad at her for making out with another guy. And it worked. I could hardly believe it. The prank worked, and they broke up, and Shawn and I dated for a while."

Tiana paused for a second but never tore her gaze from a spot on the floor. "I've changed since then, though. Obviously Shawn and I weren't meant for each other. I figured that out months ago. But when I saw Anna freak out this year, I couldn't stop thinking about what I'd done to Darla last year. She was basically sexually assaulted because of me, and I felt so guilty. I couldn't wait any longer to apologize. She'd already gone home, so I left the party and asked her to meet me on the bluff. It's where we would always hang out when we were actually friends. She walked from home and met me there, and we got to talking."

She took another breath and finally shifted her eyes but not enough to look at me. "It was when I admitted what I did last year that it happened. We were sitting on the tailgate of my truck. I explained to her how I was the one who blindfolded her and put her in the closet, how I did it on purpose to get Shawn. I thought for sure she'd forgive me because I was being honest. I was naïve to think we could go back to being friends."

Tiana shook off a shudder. "It was then that she attacked me."

I had remained silent this entire time, but I couldn't keep my question from breaking through my lips. "*She* attacked *you*?"

Tiana finally looked at me and nodded. "I told you, it was an accident. Anyway, she attacked me. The next thing I knew, I was on the gravel and she was on top of me. I remember screaming when I hit the ground. She was yelling at me, 'Do you have any idea what you've done?' and all that. I tried to shove her off and tell her I didn't do anything, but she just kept clawing at my dress. She's all like, 'He assaulted me in that closet. I lost my boyfriend and half my friends.' I was like, 'I didn't mean it,' but she didn't listen.

"I finally managed to get her off of me, and I tried running back to the truck. I mean, it was useless trying to reconcile with her. And then she pulled my hair, and I was on the ground again. I screamed, and then she kicked me and was on top of me again, pulling my hair, and I screamed again. After a struggle, I managed to somehow flip her to the ground and get on top of her, but she was choking me, and even though I was on top,

I couldn't pull away from her. She had me too tight."

Tiana's eyes glistened with tears. I wasn't sure how much I believed her, and I knew she was a good actress. Could she be making it up? Except, the three screams fit my memory, and if it happened like she said, then when I saw Darla's head hit the ground behind the bush, it must have been when Tiana got on top of her.

"I thought I was going to die," Tiana continued. "I saw the rock next to me, and I managed to grab it. I didn't mean to kill her. I was just trying to get her to stop choking me. She didn't let go, so I hit her again. Then…Oh, my God. It was horrible. It was just like…all the life drained from her eyes."

Real tears now welled up in Tiana's eyes. I almost felt for her, but I couldn't, not when I knew what she'd done. Even if it was an accident, she had still handled the situation wrong. At the very least, she could have called the cops after it all happened.

"What about her body, Tiana?" I asked in a stern tone. "What happened next?"

"Well, I couldn't let anyone find out what happened," she insisted, like I was supposed to feel sorry for her. "It would ruin my life. So I tried to move her, only she was so heavy. So I called Shawn. We were still friends, and he was the only one who would understand that it was an accident. He would keep my secret safe and protect me."

"What happened to her after that?" My own curiosity burned.

Tiana swallowed and spoke quietly. "We drove to the cemetery and buried her there with the rock. We figured it was as good a place as any to bury someone. We gathered some leaves and sprinkled them over the grave so no one would notice it was freshly dug."

I forced my shaking hands to steady. That cemetery had been giving me the creeps lately. Maybe there was a reason for that.

"And then we had one more stop to make," Tiana continued. "I snuck into Darla's room and left the note there, saying she was running away with her boyfriend. I made him up because I figured that if her family thought she was happy, they wouldn't go looking for her."

Finally, it all made sense.

"It was easy," Tiana admitted. "We'd been best friends forever, so I could copy her handwriting like it was nothing. She'd run away before, so it was perfect cover, and no one would suspect anything."

"Well, they did," I told her bluntly.

"Who? How did you find out?" Tiana pressed her lips together. "It was Shawn, wasn't it? He told Savannah, and she told you. I told him his penis would cloud his judgement."

The phrase sounded too familiar, like I'd heard her say that before. Then I remembered that I had. It was the day I caught her talking to Shawn in the hallway, when she said she "owned" him. She was threatening him about telling Savannah because they were dating.

Tiana's expression shifted. "You can't tell anyone. You know that, right? Now that you know it was an accident, that Darla attacked me, you can't turn me in. You'll help me, won't you?" Tiana stood and gripped onto my biceps, looking me in the eyes as if begging me. "And if Savannah told you, she has to know it was an accident, too. You know I didn't mean it, right? I can't go to jail for this. I'm not a bad person."

I pulled my arms from her grasp. Although her story had redeemed her to some extent, I still couldn't forgive her. She had it in her to murder someone, and it sure didn't seem like she felt remorse for it, more like she was only out to save herself. If she cared, she would have called the police. She would have let Darla's family hold a proper funeral for her. She would have let them put closure to what had happened to her. But she was too selfish for that. She didn't deserve to get off without punishment.

"I'm sorry," I told her.

"No!" Tiana cried. Tears actually began falling down her cheeks. "You can't tell anyone! I didn't mean it."

"I'm sorry," I said again, taking a step back to distance myself from her.

It was at that moment that the dressing room door finally burst open. "Okay, I've heard enough," Jack said as he pushed into the room and headed toward Tiana. "Tiana King, you're under arrest."

Tiana began crying hysterically. "No! Please. I

swear. I'm innocent. It was self-defense!"

I watched Jack drag her out of the dressing room while reading her rights to her. I was sure I had to go down to the station at some point and explain my involvement and what I heard. At least I could chalk it up to rumors and overhearing Shawn's confession. No one would have to know about my gift.

That thought made me breathe a sigh of relief. Maybe now that I knew the whole story, I could put closure to this whole ordeal. Perhaps I'd be able to astral travel again.

I didn't have much time to think about that because a few moments later, Savannah burst into the dressing room. "Oh. My. God!"

25

Savannah brushed her brown hair out of her face. "That was…There are no words!"

I nervously sank down into the chair Tiana had just been sitting in. The impact of the situation finally hit me. "What was it like out there?" I asked, gesturing to the hallway. "Everyone must have heard it." I glanced at Tiana's microphone that she'd set on the counter.

"Don't worry. Tyler already turned it off after Jack came in."

I let out the tension in my shoulders. "Good to know."

"Anyway," Savannah said, pulling a chair up across from me. "It was so surreal. Everyone heard you talk over the speakers, and they all just kind of stopped. People sat back down in the chairs, like they thought it was part of the play or something. I was outside in the receiving line, but they'd opened the doors, so I could hear. When we—all the actors—heard what was going on, we kind of crowded around the auditorium doors to listen." She shifted in her chair like she couldn't wait to tell me the rest. "When Tiana confessed, the whole place went silent for a second, and then this murmur went across the whole auditorium. Except no one moved. No one tried to stop it. I guess we all wanted to hear more."

I swallowed. "So, then what happened?"

"Well, when she ratted out Shawn, he ran. He jumped over the chairs and ran. That's when Officer Roberts chased him down and tackled him."

I recognized the officer's name but didn't really know the guy. All I knew was that he worked with Jack and they were friends. "Officer Roberts was here?"

Savannah nodded. "He must have come with Jack. They were sitting next to each other." She shifted again. "So, like I was saying, he tackled Shawn, and then when he was dragging him away, Shawn locked eyes on me and was all like, 'You promised!' Of course, I wanted to say something, but I mean, everything else was so silent. I think no one knew how to react.

"At this point, Jack was already down the hall. I guess he wanted to see how much Tiana would confess, so he waited. Then everyone heard him come in, and that's when the auditorium kind of broke apart. People started shouting. Some were like, 'She should rot in jail!' Others were like, 'It was self-defense.' That's really all I heard, though. I ran through the auditorium and signaled to Tyler in the sound booth to turn the microphone off. Now, here I am telling you all about it."

I rubbed my eyes. "Wow. I can't believe any of this. I'm sorry I did this whole thing before telling Jack. I just…She deserved it."

Savannah shook her head. "No, it's fine. We didn't have to cancel, and Tiana got what she deserved. Shawn will, too. I still can't believe he helped her. And to think, I dated him!"

"You say that like you're already over him."

Savannah's voice softened. "Far from it, but I am starting to regret ever going out with him in the first place. Thank God it never turned *serious*."

I pressed my fingers to the corners of my eyes. "I just don't know what's going to happen next." Questions raced through my mind. What would happen if I walked out into the auditorium? Would people bombard me with questions? What about after that? Would I get my gift back? "I think I should wait until everyone leaves. I'm not sure I want to see what's going on out there."

"That's fair," Savannah agreed.

Just then, a few female actors entered the dressing room. Some of them congratulated me for my courage. Others asked how I knew all I did. Some others simply gave me the evil eye, like they thought Tiana didn't deserve what I'd done to her.

"What are we going to do now?" a girl named

Hayley, who had given me the evil eye, asked no one in particular.

"What do you mean?" Savannah replied.

Hayley shrugged. "Is this it? Are we done, then? Tiana was our lead. We can't go ahead without a Cinderella."

Everyone in the dressing room just sort of froze, as if they'd all realized the same thing at that moment. They weren't going to be able to continue the play. It wasn't like they had an understudy.

That's when I realized that they practically *did*.

"You have a Cinderella," I pointed out.

Hayley eyed me. "What do you mean?"

"Savannah knows all the lines and lyrics. You won't miss an extra woodland creature. She can play Cinderella."

Savannah's eyes widened beside me like I'd just had the best idea in the world, even though she's the one who had suggested it earlier at Amberg Hamburg. Hayley's skeptical expression didn't waver, although other girls seemed interested.

"Whatever," Hayley said, turning away from us. "We'll have to see what Mr. Spears says. I'm going to bet the play is cancelled for good."

I wasn't so sure.

After the audience had dispersed, Mr. Spears called a meeting in the greenroom. We held a moment of silence for Darla before Mr. Spears spoke.

"Well," he started as the cast and crew looked up at

him from their chairs expectantly. "I have to say, that was a more eventful opening night than I thought it would be."

"What do we do now?" one of the male actors asked.

"Honestly," Mr. Spears said, "I have no idea. We may have to cancel future performances."

A groan traveled around the room. Of course, people felt for Darla—and even a few people were shedding tears for her—but they also didn't want to cancel the play.

"Why would we cancel?" a girl named Elaina asked. "Kai says Savannah knows the Cinderella role. The show must go on, right?"

Mr. Spears pivoted on his heel and aimed his gaze at Savannah. "You know *all* the lines?"

Savannah nodded but didn't reply as enthusiastically as I would have expected. No doubt losing her boyfriend the way she had was still weighing heavy on her mind. "I do. I can run through it with you if you want me to."

Mr. Spears pressed his lips together in thought. "Okay. Meet with me after this. For everyone else, plan on coming in tomorrow at the same time. I will try to get ahold of everyone if we cancel, but if you don't hear anything, we're still on. Elaina is right. The show must go on."

I swear I was just as excited as Savannah was when she finally landed her first lead role.

She perked up after the cast and crew meeting and gave me a tight hug. "I can't believe this. I actually get to play the lead! Granted, it's not under the best of circumstances, but I swear I'll be the best Cinderella there ever was."

I smiled back at her and told her with all sincerity, "I think you will be."

She hugged me one more time before heading off toward the stage to meet with Mr. Spears about her new role.

I gathered my belongings from the dressing room and slumped back through the auditorium in a daze. By now, the auditorium was empty. That's why I was surprised to hear someone call my name before I reached the doors.

I turned to find Collin closing the distance between us. "You're still here?"

He nodded. "Well, actually, I left for a while. I stopped by your house, but you weren't there, so I figured you were still here. I just wanted to say thank you."

How long had it been? It must have been at least an hour since Tiana's arrest.

I blinked a few times, trying to wake myself up from my daze. "Honestly, I still can't believe it happened."

Collin pushed a hand through his brown hair. "I can hardly believe it, either." He shifted his weight between his feet. "As evil as this might sound, I'm kind of glad we exposed her in front of everyone."

I pressed my lips together to stifle my grin. "It's oddly satisfying, isn't it?"

A smile broke across Collin's face, reassuring me that I hadn't dreamt the events of the last several hours.

"Mind if I walk you home?" Collin asked. He began walking without waiting for an answer.

I fell into step beside him. "So, what did you do when you left?"

"Huh?" His gaze darted my way for a second.

"I mean, after the play. You said you left then came back to talk to me."

Collin shoved his hands in his pocket and nodded. "Yeah, I went home and talked to my dad. I sat him down and told him everything that happened. He almost didn't believe me at first, but then I guess word got out, which doesn't surprise me. While we were talking, two people called to offer their condolences." Collin glanced around the school halls, but when he didn't see anyone around, he continued. "I wouldn't admit this to just anyone, but my dad actually started *crying*."

Collin slowed his step, and I stopped to face him. Although I would expect nothing less from a father who just found out his daughter was dead, I couldn't picture Collin's dad crying. Apparently that thought was written all over my face.

"I know, right?" Collin asked rhetorically. "I've never seen him cry before, though he wouldn't admit he was crying." He shrugged again and then turned to walk out the school doors. "He just told me to leave. I think he wanted to be alone, you know?"

Chilly air hit me when I walked outside into the night. "I can understand that."

"Anyway, I didn't know what else to do. My dad basically kicked me out of the house so he could grieve in private, so I came to find you."

"Don't you have any other friends?" I asked before I could stop myself. I knew it sounded rude the moment it escaped my mouth, but I didn't mean it in that way.

Collin laughed lightly. "Of course I have other friends, but it's different with you. I can talk to you about this stuff, and you won't judge me."

"I'm sorry," I started, but he cut me off.

"No, I get it. We only started talking a few weeks ago, and here I am bearing my soul to you. It's just, we've kind of been in this together, and I don't think my other friends would quite understand."

I liked the way he said "other friends" like he considered me one of his friends.

"So," I started, fiddling with my backpack strap, "do you know what's going to happen now?"

He fell silent for a second, and I almost thought he wasn't going to answer, but then he spoke. "I have no idea. I imagine Tiana and Shawn will go to jail. Someone will probably come to our house in the morning—or maybe they're already there talking to my dad. I've been thinking about the funeral." Collin stared into the distance when he said the word "funeral." I could only imagine how painful this was for him.

I didn't even want to think about holding Braden's funeral. If he died tomorrow, I knew I'd regret never telling my brother that I loved him.

"How are you doing?" I asked Collin sympathetically.

He took a deep breath but didn't slow his pace. "Honestly, I feel kind of relieved. I mean, I'm sad she's gone. More than sad. It's not something I can really express in words. But at the same time, I now know what happened to her, and at least now my dad and I can put her to rest."

I suspected Collin had his own way of grieving for his sister. That, or he had already done enough grieving for her in the past two weeks. Either way, he didn't cry in front of me, though I wouldn't have blamed him if he did.

We reached my house almost too soon. I stood at the door awkwardly staring at my feet.

"So, uh." Collin cleared his throat.

I tucked a loose strand of red hair that had escaped from my ponytail behind my ear. "Yeah?"

"You still owe me that race." Finally, the tension eased.

I smiled. "I do. I have to work tomorrow morning, but I already took off work early for the play. We could meet when I get off work…" My voice trailed off when I noticed the way he was staring at me with soft eyes and a hint of a smile. His gaze shifted to my lips. They twitched uncontrollably under his stare, and my mouth went dry.

Just when I thought he was leaning in, my ringtone cut through the silence, startling me. I flushed in embarrassment when I jumped. Thankfully, the porch light wasn't on, so it was dim enough that Collin didn't notice.

I checked my phone to find my mom was calling. I laughed at the irony. "Well, uh, I gotta go."

"I'll see you tomorrow, then."

"Yeah. I get off work at noon, and I'll need to change. Meet me here at 12:30?" I paused for a second. "That is, if you'll be available. The police might want to talk to you or something."

"I'll text you if there's a change in plans."

"Are you going to be okay tonight?" I asked.

"You mean with my dad? Yeah. I'll just creep up to my room. It will be fine." A smile crept across his face before I could turn to leave. "I'll see you tomorrow."

"Can't wait." I smiled back before pushing through my front door and unwillingly leaving Collin alone in the dark.

26

"I'm home!" I announced when I entered the door.

My mother stood in the kitchen with the landline phone in her hand. She set it on the base when she met my gaze. "Oh, good. I was just about to call you again. Are you okay?"

"So, you heard?" I already knew the answer to that question based on her inflection.

"Jack told me."

I slumped into a chair at the table. "He came over?"

My mother furrowed her brow and situated herself in her own chair in front of a pile of papers. "Why do you say it like that?"

I blinked a few times. "What do you mean?"

"You say it like you're upset that Jack comes over."

I pressed my lips together. The truth was, I wasn't

happy about it, but could I tell her that? I swallowed the guilt in my throat. I couldn't continue to hide my feelings from her. In a second, she could be gone, just like Darla, and I'd regret it forever. "That's because I am upset," I confessed.

My mother tilted her head in confusion. "Why?"

I bit my lip and refused to meet her gaze. I couldn't believe I'd just admitted that to her. My mom and I didn't exactly talk about things, but now that the confession was out, I couldn't take it back. "It's just…you don't seem to ever have time for Braden and me. You'll have even less time for us if you start dating Jack."

After a silent beat, my mother burst out laughing.

I widened my eyes at her. What was she laughing about? The sound was so strange. I couldn't remember the last time I'd heard my mom laugh like that with me.

"You think I like Jack?" She said it like it was a ridiculous notion.

Wait. Was it? "You mean, you don't?" I asked slowly.

"Kai, I'm not going to date Jack. I assure you of that."

"Then why does he visit all the time? What's with the haircut and the cooking and all of that?"

My mother snickered. "It certainly wasn't because I want to *date* him."

"Oh." I shifted in my chair. That news left me a bit more comfortable.

"It's actually something I've been meaning to talk to you about, but I didn't want to tell you until I was sure I had the money. I wanted it to be a surprise."

"The money for what?" My gaze drifted down to the pile of papers in front of my mom.

She picked up an envelope that was on top of the pile and slid it across the table. I eyed it. What was going on?

"Jack has been helping me for the last couple of months. Most of the time, you were at work or on your run when he visited. But it's not because we're dating. He's been helping me with our finances. The haircut, the cooking, it was all my way of paying him back for his help."

Relief washed over me. *That* made sense, and it was a whole lot better than my mom *dating* him.

"So, what's this?" I reached out for the envelope.

"Go ahead." My mom smiled. "Open it."

I did, and when I peeled back the seal, I could hardly believe my eyes. My nose tingled at the threat of tears. All this time I thought my mom didn't care, that she had no regard for me, but here she was, paying me back. I pulled the stack of money out of the envelope without saying a word.

"That's all the money I borrowed from you. Jack has helped me enough that I've been able to get caught up on some bills and save up money."

I couldn't speak as a bundle of emotions rose in my throat. I pushed up from my chair and around the table to my mom, where I pulled her into a hug.

She drew back for a moment in surprise and then melted into the embrace. "Kai, what is it?"

Tears streamed down my face. I pulled away from her to wipe them off my cheeks. "I just—" My voice cracked. "I love you, is all." I actually wasn't entirely sure what I was feeling. I felt somewhat guilty for acting so childish and assuming my mom was going to date Jack when he was only being a good friend, but I also felt grateful for all my mom had done for me, even if she always seemed busy. She must have been preoccupied lately getting our finances in order.

"I love you, too."

"What are you guys doing?" Braden's voice cut through our moment. I looked up to find him rubbing his eyes as if we'd woken him up.

I rushed around the table and threw my arms around him. Braden pushed at me, but I didn't budge.

"What are you doing?" he asked in a slightly different tone.

My emotions got the better of me, and all I could think about when I saw his face was how I couldn't bear to lose him without him knowing that I loved him. "I love you, Braden," I told him.

After a moment, he relaxed, like he realized I was serious. "Uh, I love you, too, Kai."

Mom joined our group hug. It was the first time in a long time our family felt like a family.

* * *

I quickly drifted off to sleep that night and found myself surprised at the familiar sensation of crawling out of my own body. I stood at my own bedside and stared down at my sleeping form. A moment of confusion stalled me, but when realization dawned, I couldn't help the smile that broke out across my face.

"Yes!" I shouted to myself in relief. I'd done it! I'd found the closure I needed by solving Darla's murder, and now I could astral travel again.

After a moment to relish in the glory of the situation, I realized I had hours at my fingertips to enjoy. I just needed to figure out where I was going to travel to. I rushed over to my bookshelf and reached out for my dream book, only when my hand fell through the spine, I remembered I couldn't actually grab it in the state I was in. Where was it that I had planned to travel after Yalong Bay? I couldn't remember, not because I didn't care, but over the past few days, I'd slowly thought about astral traveling less and less, like there was more to me now than just my gift.

Now that I could astral travel again, where would I go? I wasn't exactly as sour about Amberg as I had been a few weeks ago, and my family and I had made up on some level, so I didn't feel like rushing away from them, either; although, there were other people and places I wanted to see. That thought left me focused on one thing. I closed my eyes. When I opened them, I found myself standing in front of Collin's house. I wasn't sure exactly what I was doing there.

My heart pounded as I looked up at the second-story windows. I couldn't spy on him, could I? That'd be an invasion of privacy, and what if he wasn't in bed yet? What if I caught him getting dressed?

At the same time, I felt a pull toward the house, to Collin, and a sort of curiosity overcame me. I guiltily stepped toward the house, on one level not wanting to invade Collin's privacy, but on another knowing I wouldn't be caught.

I walked through the door with ease. The house was dim and eerily quiet, but even in the dark, it was just as beautiful inside as I had imagined. I crept up the stairs without making a sound, and I took a guess as to which room was Collin's. I paused outside of it, wanting desperately to go in but not sure if I should. I'd never been to someone's house in my spiritual state before. It felt like I was breaking and entering. But I couldn't stop myself now.

I stepped through the door and immediately heard a voice. I almost thought I'd been caught, like he could see me, but as I continued to listen to Collin's words, I realized he was praying. So this was how he dealt with his sister's death.

"God," he whispered to thin air. I never knew Collin was religious, but something about the way he was kneeling at his bedside with his hands folded together made me want to sit beside him and pray, too. "I miss my sister," he admitted, "but I know she's in a better place now and that you'll take care of her."

I should go, I thought to myself. It was wrong to eavesdrop on someone else's prayers. I closed my eyes, ready to conjure up another location, but the next words out of Collin's mouth stopped me.

"I'm thankful that you sent me Kai."

My eyes shot open in surprise before I could transport my spirit elsewhere. I paused to listen.

"I know you've blessed me with plenty of friends, but there's something different about Kai. I can talk to her in a way that I can't with anyone else. She came just at the right time. She helped me find my sister's killer, and when everything feels like it's falling apart, she seems to hold me together somehow. I can still joke and smile and laugh around her, and I just wanted to thank you for blessing me with her in my life."

Tears began welling up in my eyes. Without consciously deciding to, I crossed the room and knelt beside him. I couldn't take my gaze off his face. I wanted to look into his eyes, to tell him everything was going to be alright, but they were closed.

"God, I don't know what would have happened if I hadn't changed my route that first day I ran into Kai on the bluff. I know now that it was your hand that guided me to her, to convince me to run the new route every day so I could find her there waiting for me."

Wait. He purposely adjusted his route so he could meet up with me? I didn't know what to think of that in the slightest, though I certainly wasn't bothered by it.

"Heavenly Father," he continued, "please grant me

the strength to work through my sister's death according to your plan. Help me to be strong when people ask me questions about it. Help me to plan my sister's funeral and to help support my father as we go through this trial together. And please, God, tell my sister I love her. Amen."

I was too stunned to move. Even after Collin opened his eyes and situated himself into bed, I didn't budge for a long time. I just sat at his bedside and watched him sleep. I knew it was wrong to listen in on his prayers—heck, I was a creep for watching him sleep—but I didn't regret it.

After a long while of watching Collin's chest rise and fall and his eyes move under his lids, I stood and exited his room. I wasn't quite sure what I'd do at this point, but as I passed another door in the hallway, curiosity got the better of me.

I stepped into Darla's bedroom, which was lit by the soft glow of the street lamp outside her window. It was pristine, but each corner of the room held a symbol of Darla's personality. Photos of her and her friends and family hung on her mirror and bulletin board. I noticed there weren't any of Tiana or Shawn. Darla was all smiles in her pictures. In one, she had donned ski gear and stood at the top of a mountain. In another, she held a ribbon next to Collin after completing a 5K together. I recognized Poas Volcano in the background of one of the photos. I had visited Costa Rica while traveling during one of my mid-day naps, and Poas Volcano was one of my stops. I didn't feel a pang of jealousy when I noticed the photo, though, only joy that Darla got to see it in person before her death.

I turned from the photographs. Across the room, one wall housed hand-drawn photos tacked to the wall in a colorful array. Yet another wall was dedicated to snow globes. I remembered how Collin said she collected them.

I took my time and investigated each snow globe and wondered about the significance of each. Even after I'd inspected each visible element in the room, I simply stood there, briefly wondering what life was like for her and where she'd be right now if she was still alive. Still, I couldn't help but notice how much life and personality there was in this room. Though Darla had been hurt this past year by back-stabbing friends, there was clearly joy in parts of her life. It was unfair that her life was taken so soon, but at least she got to experience it. I didn't know if there was a god out there, but after hearing Collin's prayer, I sure hoped that Darla was in a better place like Collin had said.

I paused at Darla's door before exiting. "Goodbye, Darla."

27

"I thought you weren't coming into work today," Meg's voice rang out from behind me.

"Oh, I'm not working," I told her, turning from the products I was browsing.

I'd been called to the police station this morning for questioning, so I had to take off work last-minute. Mom had to come along since I was a minor, but it wasn't as scary as I thought it'd be. Like I'd hoped, I blamed my knowledge on gossip and overhearing Shawn, and they bought it. It's not like they would buy the alternative, though, that I was magically in two places at the same time. Maybe one day I would tell someone about my abilities, but I decided that day wasn't today.

At least Jack believed everything I'd told him. He didn't know I was lying again, but he believed me enough that it almost felt like he'd forgiven me for my prior lies of being kidnapped. He even apologized for not listening to me to begin with.

"Oh," Meg said, pulling me from my thoughts. "So, what are you doing here?"

"I just needed to pick up a few ingredients. I'm making my mom's mashed potatoes for dinner. She puts French dip with bacon in it so it tastes like baked potatoes."

Meg smacked her lips. "Sounds delicious."

"It is." I smiled. "But I'm kind of in a rush."

"Hot date?" she joked.

My cheeks flushed at the thought. Was it a date? "Kind of," I admitted. The thought of Collin immediately reminded me of our deal to eat a tub of vanilla ice cream together.

Meg grinned back at me. "Well, if you're almost ready, I can ring you up."

"Thanks, Meg." I met her at the cash register after taking a detour to the freezer aisle for ice cream. I approached her, giddy with excitement, not only about seeing Collin shortly, but about surprising my family with dinner. They were going to love it!

* * *

I arrived home closer to 12:30 than I would have liked. I stashed my ingredients in the kitchen and then rushed off to my room to change into my running gear. Just as I finished tying my shoes, the doorbell rang, and my heart leapt in my chest.

I quickly made my way to the door and found exactly what I expected to behind it: Collin. I thought back to last night, about what he'd said about me in his prayers, and my face flushed. After a moment, I remembered that he had no idea I'd heard it all, and I forced myself to relax.

"Ready?" Collin asked.

"Ready to kick your butt, you mean? I'm definitely up for it."

He laughed. "So, did you have to talk to the police this morning?"

I nodded as I pushed my way onto the porch and shut the door behind me. "Did you?"

"Yeah."

"How'd it go? Okay?" I asked.

"I guess so. It wasn't as nerve-racking as I thought it would be."

"That's good to hear. So, what route are we taking?" I gazed down the street to get an idea of where we should go.

"How about whoever gets to the bluff first wins?" Collin offered.

"You're on." Before we could even shake on it, Collin had taken off. "Hey," I called after him, pushing my legs to catch up. "You could have warned me."

"That would be too easy," he called back.

I sprinted forward until we were running side-by-side. As we ran farther, he pushed ahead of me, but I wasn't going to let some guy with a bad ankle beat me. Yet I couldn't seem to catch up to him, always maintaining the same distance no matter how fast I ran. We soon reached the bottom of the bluff, and that's when I gave it my all. By the time we made it the top, we were side-by-side again.

Collin fell down into the grass in the clearing near our running trail. "That was close. I have no idea who won."

I sprawled next to him, and a few leaves crunched under my weight. "What do you say we call it a tie?" I suggested, even though I was pretty sure I actually won by a split second, but I didn't want to gloat.

"If you keep running like that, you have a good chance of bringing home some titles next year in cross country. You are going to sign up, aren't you?"

I tilted my head toward him, but the shine in his eyes didn't help slow my heart rate. "Yeah, I really think I will."

Collin pushed himself to his feet. "We should walk it off. Don't want your muscles tightening up after a run like that."

I knew that was the best idea, even though I didn't want to move right now. Still, I found my way to my feet and paced beside him. After a few minutes, Collin stopped at the guardrail near the edge of the cliff. He leaned his elbows on the rotting wood.

"Why do they even bother with this thing?" I asked absentmindedly. "It's not like it stops anyone from climbing over it."

Collin pressed his lips together like he was thinking.

"No one gets in trouble, either." I remembered the four boys who had scared me by cliff jumping.

"You're right," he said before swinging his legs over the top board.

"Oh, my God! What are you doing?"

Collin paced to the edge of the cliff and shot back a menacing grin.

"You could fall!"

His smile grew. "Come on." He held his hand out to me like he expected me to follow.

Part of me wanted to, but I was still frightened of the edge. How terrible could it be, though? I'd hung my feet off the cliff plenty of times in my spiritual state, and it wasn't that frightening. Besides, people jumped off the cliff. It's not like the fall would hurt me — apparently the river was deep enough and slow enough not to.

"Are you sure about this?" I asked warily, not crossing the guardrail line even though part of me wanted to.

"Remember when you told me you wanted to get out of Amberg so you could travel? You said you wanted to skydive and things like that." Collin never dropped his inviting hand.

I nodded.

"You realize you don't have to wait to start experiencing the world, don't you?"

I furrowed my brow. "I literally have no idea what you mean."

"You need to stop waiting around for something to happen to you. You need to *make* it happen."

Dang, this guy made a lot of sense. Okay. I could do this. If dangling my feet off the edge was the first step to seeing the world, I was willing to do it. I reached out for Collin's hand and crossed the barrier. Collin grinned and began unlacing his shoes.

Nerves shuddered through my body. "What are you doing?"

He looked up at me from his crouch. "Well, I'm not jumping in with my shoes on."

"We're *jumping* in?" I exclaimed. I had assumed we were only going to sit on the edge. That was freaky enough. I didn't think I could actually jump.

Collin slipped off his socks and shoes, and then he stood beside me. He held onto my wrists lightly and stared into my eyes. "Kai, you can do this. You want adventure in life. You told me so, and I can see it in your eyes."

I glanced toward the edge of the cliff. It seemed a longer way down in real life. "I don't know if I really want that," I admitted. "Maybe I don't really want to skydive."

"That's a lie," Collin accused.

Maybe it was. I had only ever traveled in my dreams as an observer. I never truly experienced adventure, and the thought of diving head-first into it at this very moment sent adrenaline coursing through my blood. Only, I realized, that was the point, wasn't it? But did I like it? Did I want this type of adventure, or was I content in my passive travels?

"Try it just once," Collin pleaded. "You'll never know if you enjoy the adventure if you don't take a shot at it. If it scares you, you don't ever have to do it again. If you like it, we can go on more adventures."

"We?" I asked almost too quickly.

Collin shrugged, never distancing himself from me, although I wasn't going to argue with his proximity. "Why not? We could do so much together."

"Like what?"

"Well, for starters, junior prom?"

Oh, my God! Did Collin just ask me to prom? Excitement immediately overtook my mind. That was months away, and he was brave enough to ask me so early, like he thought we'd still be friends by then? Something inside of me knew that we would, and I could already picture myself in a purple silk dress dancing in Collin's arms.

My voice came out barely audible. "That sounds like an adventure."

Neither of us spoke another word. In the next instant, Collin's lips met mine unexpectedly. Butterflies came to life in my stomach, and while parts of my body tensed in exhilaration, my lips relaxed to melt into his. I couldn't breathe, but it didn't matter. In that moment, all that mattered were Collin's lips, and they were mine now.

He pulled away too soon, but I didn't have to think twice. I slipped my shoes and socks off in record time and reached for Collin's hand. I positioned myself toward the edge of the cliff and shot him a glance of approval.

And then I leapt into my next adventure.

ABOUT THE AUTHOR

Alicia Rades is a USA Today bestselling author of young adult paranormal fiction with a love for supernatural stories set in the modern world. When she's not plotting out fiction novels, you can find her writing content for various websites or plowing her way through her never-ending reading list. Alicia holds a bachelor's degree in communications with an emphasis on professional writing.